What God Brings Together

Promises from Above Series Book 1

Melissa Wardwell

1

Cover Design: Diane McKay
Cover Image: Victorine Lieske

"And the two shall become one flesh; so they are no longer two, but one flesh. What therefore God has joined together, let no man separate."
Mark 10:8-9 (HCSB)

Prologue

Ryan put his shoes on as he watched his boys, Stephen and Aaron. They were playing with their toy cars on the living room floor. Ryan could not be more proud. He never dreamed he would have a family. He was a bit of a loner when he had met his wife and he had resigned himself to the idea of never marrying or having children. He was okay with the notion of coming and going as he pleased and not being tied down. Now, he could never imagine his life without them. He counted his blessings every day. He felt as though he had been given more than he deserved.

Stephen, who was five, was a lot like Ryan - laid back and quiet. The boy had his mama's looks though. He was Ryan's little buddy. He liked cars, motorcycles and fishing. Aaron, who was three, acted much like Emma- curious and funny, but resembled Ryan just a bit. He had to admit, he had a hard time relating with his youngest son. He could tell already he would be an artsy kid who liked to draw and color. His boys amazed him daily in their differences.

"Tickle me daddy!" yelled Stephen while jumping up and down waving his chubby arms. Having a couple of minutes before he had to leave for work, he figured, *why not?* With a deep growl, Ryan attacked - rolling around on the floor and tickling his boys. The three of them were being so loud that no one heard the tiny holler coming from the bedroom at the end of the hall, but his beautiful wife, Emma, did.

"Come on! Can't I get a half an hour of rest?" he heard her say from their bedroom.

"Daddy, you woked Sawa," stated Aaron in his broken grammar. "Mama not happy." Leave it to Aaron to point out his mistakes.

Sarah was only 3 weeks old and Emma was trying to get a "power nap" in before Ryan left for work. Second shift was not a good shift for the family, but what choice did he have. He hated that he couldn't even help her with the boys during the craziest part of the day. He got up to go get the baby, his sweet princess, but Emma got to the room before he could.

"I am sorry baby. I wasn't thinking." He told her when they meet at the nursery door.

"Clearly! Just go ahead and go to work, I can manage from here. Just drive safe and have a good day." Then she gave him a chaste kiss on the cheek and turned away to tend to baby Sarah's needs.

He thought his wife was amazing and her ability to multitask left him in awe every time he watched her, but wondered often if she really even needed him. He felt like the proverbial third wheel in his own family most of the time. Rarely did she ask for his help with the kids or chores. Was his only purpose in life to work and bring home a good paycheck?

He walked up behind her and slipped his arms around her waist from behind and whispered in her ear, "You are an amazing woman, you know that? I love you, babe." He kissed her on the temple and stepped back a bit with his hand still on her waist, "I'll put in a movie and make a snack for the boys before I go." She responded with a whispered, "Thank you" and kept changing Sarah.

There was so much he wanted to say to her, but he figured if he said anything else it would make her more upset right now. He knew that much of her mood was a lack of sleep and stress, he tried to be understanding. Some days were just harder than others.

Once the boys had settled, he kissed their little heads and told them good-bye. With a heavy sigh, Ryan walked to the truck and to go to work. *There has to be more. I go to work, come home, sleep, get up, eat, and head for work again. There has to be more to this life, Lord. You blessed me with a beautiful, amazing wife and three awesome kids, and I can't even enjoy them right now.*

The drive was long so he always had time to think about things like how bills were piling up and what was going on at home. Today, all he could do was worry about Emma and how she spread herself so thin taking care of them.

Their six year wedding anniversary was coming up in a month and he wanted to do something really special. What he would like to do, what he could financially do, and what he knew she needed were all things to consider. Whatever they did, he wanted it to be special. He thought maybe a weekend getaway would be a good idea but with Sarah so young, he wasn't sure how that would work.

Then the idea to have her mom come for a visit for a week or two came to mind. He knew Emma would enjoy seeing her mother again.

His in-laws lived on the other side of the state where they had bought a retirement home on the edge of Lake Michigan two years before. Her mom had been able to help out with the boys because they had lived a block away before, but not this time. He knew it would not be ideal for an anniversary gift. He didn't mind though, Emma needed a break.

Emma was such a blessing to him. From the moment he first laid eyes on her from down the hall in high school, he was taken by her. Her ice blue eyes danced every time she smiled while talking with her friends and it just drew him in more.

They did not move in the same "social circles" but he just had to get to know her. She was active in her church youth group which told him they believed in the same thing. She sang in the choir and he could only imagine that she sounded like an angel. He found out later that he was right. She was kind and outgoing. She did well in school. The thought had crossed his mind a few times to see if she could tutor him in something, anything, as long as he could get to know her better.

After the Christmas break of their sophomore year, he had finally gotten up the nerve to talk to her, but only because she was transferred into his history class. That had to be God working because they never did mid-year transfers. After a couple of weeks of watching her across the classroom, he finally had the courage to say hello. As he walked toward the empty desk behind her, fear and uncertainty crept in. He remembered thinking back then that he didn't stand a chance with her. He had not been a jock or an overly smart student. He had felt like he didn't have much to offer her.

He smiled as he reminisced about the brief conversation they had that fateful day.

"Hi! I'm Ryan," he said as he started to sit down.

She turned to look at him. "I'm Emma", she said with a smile.

"You don't mind me sitting here, do you?"

"No one else is in a hurry to. Go ahead."

"You transferred in here midterm. How did you manage that?"

"My math class was a little too much for me, so they had to shift my schedule around a bit to get me in an easier class. Math is not my strong point."

"Well, I just happen to be a math whiz," he said with a cocky grin. "I can tutor you a bit if you would like."

"Oh, that would be great! My dad would like it too. He has been helping me, but I think I frustrate him a bit."

"Great! How about..."

"Okay class, how about we get started?" interrupted the teacher.

"Will you meet me at lunch?" he asked in a whisper.

"Sure, I would like that." *OH YEA!!! God, can I please have her?* He silently prayed as he sat back in his seat with a grin that spanned his face from ear to ear.

A car headed in his direction driving in his lane pulled him from the memory. He shook his head to focus at what was going on, the car crossed the center line to pass a tractor and clearly hadn't thought to look for oncoming traffic. Ryan swerved to miss the car but hit the tractor instead. Just as Ryan's head hit the steering wheel, all he could think was *God, not yet!* The lights faded away as he slipped into blackness.

Ryan came to a couple moments later, but barely. He had a hard time opening his right eye and he couldn't move to crawl out because his seat belt was locked and wouldn't come undone. He felt panic build up in his chest as he frantically tried to reach for anything he could to get out but had very little luck. He could move his left arm so he slowly raised his hand to touch his face and felt the sticky wetness of blood but something didn't feel right. He could feel a massive slash down the right side of his face along with many other smaller cuts.

His attention to his face shifted to the sudden heat coming up from his feet. *WOW! It is getting hot in here. Who turned on the furnace? What is going on?* As the pain started to set in, he realized the car was on fire. He could smell the smoke and burning of tires and motor oil.

"HELP!" he tried to yell. His voice felt strained.

The faint sound of boots on the pavement coming his way was followed by a voice. "Help is coming man! Can you move?"

Then he heard the stranger curse under his breath as he frantically cut away the seat belt with his pocket knife. Ryan's head felt foggy and was spinning but he didn't care, as long as he got out. He could feel the heat of the flames move further into the car. He knew he didn't have long before it would blow up.

"Almost got it. I have to pull you out, but it is going to hurt, you ready?"

Ryan nodded as best as he could, but at that moment the flames surged to up his right side. He tried to stifle a scream of pain, and failed.

Ryan heard another curse out of his rescuer and then he said, "Here we go, I pull, you push with your feet. ONE! TWO! THREE!"

Ryan tried as best as he could to do as he was told, but he couldn't find the strength. The pain was so intense that he couldn't even think any longer. The stranger pulled him from the car and rolled Ryan in a cloth of some kind to put out the flames on his body. He hurt all over. He prayed God would let him die just to get away from the pain. He knew things were not looking good for him. He could feel the whole right side of his body begin to blister.

I have to get a message to Emma. He opened his left eye to get a quick glimpse of the man helping him. The man was in his fatigues. He knew this man was someone he could count on.

"Tell Emma..." Ryan's eye shut. He was having a hard time staying awake.

"Stay with me man, help's coming. You hear 'em? You can tell her yourself. Just hang in there."

Ryan could hear the sirens, but he knew that death was coming too.

"Tell Emma...love her." He whispered out through ragged breaths and shooting pain. In his delirium, he pleaded, "God, take me."

At that moment, there was a great explosion that rocked the ground. Ryan could feel the heat of it and it intensified the pain he was already in. He could faintly hear someone yelling in pain. It was him, he felt it in his throat, but his ears were ringing from the explosion. He grabbed at the soldier as best as he could with his left hand as he felt himself slipping away,

"Tell....Emma...Please." The darkness and silence slipped over him before he could hear the man's response.

Chapter 1

New job, new house, new school, old town. That's where she was. Sitting at her desk. The work day about to begin. Life had not been kind up to this point, but she did the best she could with what she had.

Today marked eight years since that fateful day. How Emma had gone this long without Ryan was beyond her understanding, but she had. There was no choice. Stephen, Aaron and Sarah counted on her. She had to keep going, for them, but when was it enough? She was so tired of doing it on her own. Eight years of single parenthood was a hard load to bear. She just couldn't understand why God had allowed things to happen the way they had. The hardest part for her to wrap her brain around was how the days after the accident played out.

She gazed out the window of her classroom as she reminisced about the last eight years.

About an hour after Ryan had left for work that day, there was a loud knock on her front door. It was so loud that it startled Sarah. Feeling irritated at the person for waking the baby that she had just gotten to sleep, she answered the door. Before her stood a police officer and a military officer. She immediately felt self-conscious because she was still in her pajamas. She saw the concern wash over their faces and she began to realize something bad happened.

"Ma'am, can we come in? I am not sure you want us to talk to you from out here." The police officer must have seen the look of bewilderment on her face. She numbly opened the door. All the common sense lessons about letting strange men in her home when she was alone fled her mind. Something had happened to her husband. They were right, it was better to do this inside.

She turned her back to the men as they entered and told the boys to go to their room. She heard the boys make comments of protest but she couldn't tell you what they said.

She looked back at the men and mumbled something about her needing to go change into some clothes. They nodded in response and she left the room she wondered about leaving the men alone but knew she needed to change her clothes and do so quickly. She took Sarah with her and checked in on the boys. They looked at her with total confusion.

As soon as she entered their bedroom, she felt the dam begin to crack. She gently placed Sarah on the bed and went about changing into the closest thing she could grab - Ryan's sweat pants and his favorite college football t-shirt. She blankly made her way back over to where she had put Sarah down. The little bundle of pink blanket laid there sleeping on Ryan's side of the bed. It was still unmade. She grabbed his pillow swiftly and inhaled his scent. The dam cracked more. She wasn't sure how much longer she could hold it in. An overwhelming feeling swept over her, one that every dream they had and their very way of life had changed drastically in the last hour.

She put the pillow down and carefully picked up their daughter. The sweet little thing was still asleep. She went down the hall to the nursery and placed Sarah back in her crib. The realization of how cruel she had been to Ryan that afternoon slapped her in the face and she felt the shame come over her. She had not been a good person to him and now she wasn't sure she would get the chance to change that. "Well girl, let's find out", she said to herself as she pulled her shoulders back and put on a brave face.

She walked out to the living room where the men had sat on the couch while they waited for her. The boys had made their way back out to the living room while she dressed and put Sarah down. "Boys, please go back to your room while mommy talks to these men." They went obediently with their heads bowed down and their lips out. They were in that phase where men in uniform were fascinating.

"Can I get you gentlemen some water?" She was trying to avoid the inevitable.

"No thank you", they said in unison.

"In fact, we need you to call someone to come and sit with the children. There has been an accident involving your husband and you're needed as soon as possible at the hospital."

She could see the compassion in the officer's eyes. She hated the look already. She decided to push it away and made a call to her sister in law, Tiffany. His parents would want to be at the hospital.

A few short minutes later, she was following the police car to the hospital. She did her best to keep a clear head. They couldn't tell her much due to privacy laws. She took comfort in the fact that they had said that last they knew; Ryan was still alive. She could handle caring for him for a while, but she wasn't sure about losing him permanently.

Summoning images that were pleasing so her mood stayed positive, she recalled the look of awe that came over the silent soldier's face when Tiffany walked in her door. The thought made Emma giggle for a moment and then she began to cry. She could feel hysteria begin to settle in. "God, I can't do this alone. Help me out here."

As they pulled into the parking lot, Ryan's parents were huddled together with his brother outside the sliding ER door. She sat there in the car watching them. She wasn't sure she could go in but knew she had to. Before she could open her car door, it opened for her and before her stood the soldier.

He knelt down in front of her. "Ma'am. I was on the scene before the EMT's were able to arrive. I pulled him from his truck. I know I probably shouldn't say anything to you but I think you need to be prepared. I also have a message from your husband." They both took a deep breath. She figured he was dreading telling her what he had to as much as she didn't want to hear it. "First of all, he said 'Tell her, love her.'

Then he lost consciousness. Second, there was a fire and explosion."

She felt the breath leave her, "Oh dear God" was her breathy response.

He touched her hand, "He was alive last I saw him, like the officer said. Your husband was burned pretty badly. I had gotten him out just seconds before the explosion. That is when he gave me the message. I think he thought...well, it doesn't matter. You need to get in there." He rose back to his full height and backed away enough for her to get out of the car. He put out his hand to help her. Once she righted herself, she looked deep into his eyes. She could see he was dealing with a few demons of his own because of this.

"What's your name? Ryan will want to know - to thank you."

"Corporal Bradley Jones, ma'am," he told her.

"Thank you for caring, Corporal."

She didn't remember walking to the doors or even walking to the nurses' station. What she did remember though was the blood curdling scream coming from one of the rooms. The nurse looked up at her with eyes as wide as saucers. It had clearly startled her as much as it did Emma.

"Um, I am here about my husband. Ryan Daniels."

The nurses behind the desk all looked at her now with pity and sorrow and then looked down the hall to where the scream had come from. She followed their glances in time to see a doctor walk toward her.

"Are you Mrs. Daniels?"

"I am," she felt hesitant to respond.

The doctor pulled her aside and told her the extent of his injuries, which he was presently sedated, and they were tending to his wounds. She then heard a gasp beside her and a large hand encase her shoulders. She looked around her and saw her in-laws were with her. Her father-in-law had her and his wife in his arms. She didn't even realize they had walked up beside her.

He had suffered serious, disfiguring third degree burns down his whole right side. He had sustained some broad lacerations on his head, face, and arms. He also had several broken ribs.

For the first week she paced the halls waiting for a change in his condition. Maybe even a chance to talk to him. Eight days after the accident, she was informed that an infection that had started in his leg. The doctors said that if it didn't clear up soon, they would have to amputate his leg just above the knee. They warned her that he would need some massive reconstructive surgery on his face. He would not look the same ever again. They had kept Ryan in a coma for weeks so that he could heal without a lot of movement. It all felt like an out of body experience to her.

The silver lining to all of this was that insurance was covering everything. So she felt blessed enough that there would be no medical bills hanging over her head. Ryan's boss had called her and told her that Ryan would still have a job to come back to when he was ready. By doing this, insurance would stay active.

She had started to believe that Corp. Jones was an angel in uniform. About a week after the accident, as she was making her way to the car one morning, she almost tripped over four sacks of groceries. She could not believe that someone would care so much. On one of the bags was a brief note, "an angel." The next week she watched out the window of the living room as she fed Sarah. She was touched to see the corporal walk up to the house with an arm-full of grocery bags. He had done that once a week for quite some time.

Those weeks were stressful for Emma and the kids. The boys didn't understand why their daddy wasn't home. They had even started to act up more than normal. The experts say babies can feel your tension, and Sarah was proving that to be true. She was constantly fussy and didn't eat well. Emma had been nursing Sarah at the time of the accident, but she could feel that her supply was starting to dry up. It didn't matter how often she pumped to keep it going, she continued to lose her milk. Sarah did not like the formula for quite a while. It hurt Emma's heart that her kids had to suffer so much.

One day, on her way to Ryan's room to sit with him, Ryan's doctor stopped her in the hall and asked if she would join him in his office. Her heart dropped to her feet. She was concerned that the infection had not improved. She didn't even remember walking into the elevator and then walking down the hall to his office. She was seated in a heavily padded, high back chair with him sitting across from her. She knew this news would be really serious if he didn't sit behind the desk like normal. She remembered the sadness in his eyes and the hesitation in his movements.

He started with telling her that Ryan was awake and that he was healing nicely. The infection was down drastically and that he was coming out of the worst of his injuries. She recalled the relief she felt and said a thank you to God for the healing that she and so many were praying for. She didn't see that same relief in the doctor's face. With a heavy sigh, he took her hands and looked her in the eyes. "He doesn't want any more visitors." She was confused by this comment. She didn't have a problem with that but then the doctor told her, "that includes family, and it includes you, Mrs. Daniels."

She couldn't believe her ears. In fact, she had no idea what he had said after that. The flood of different emotions that washed over her fell heavy on her chest. First, it was confusion, then clarity, then heartbreak, but it was when anger set in that she had stormed from the office, marched her way down the hall and to the elevator. She slammed her finger on the button that would direct her to the floor Ryan was on. Inside the elevator, she grumbled and mumbled about what a coward he was. The doors to the floor slid open and she marched her way down the hall and right into his room.

She knew he was awake because his left eye was open and he had the TV remote in his hand. He appeared to be watching TV. She stood at the end of his bed, happy to see he was awake, but still furious at him. She crossed her arms over her chest and cocked one hip up and glared at him. He should have seen her because she was standing in front of the TV he was watching, but he didn't respond. He just looked right through her. The right side of his face was bandaged up like the rest of his body. He looked so helpless. Seeing him like this softened her heart a little bit, enough so that she didn't yell at him. But she was still mad.

"You won't see me? I'm your wife!?" Nothing. He didn't say a word.

"Why? Why would you make a request like that? I don't understand Ryan!" She was at his side. She looked at him, but he didn't indicate in any way that he had heard her. The only move he made was to close his eye and turn his head away from her. All she had seen then was the back of his head. She was beyond mad. She wanted to continue with a verbal vengeance, but he had shut her out. She had no understanding of why. No explanation. He had indicated to her that he was done and was not going to explain himself. She was stunned by his response. She turned to leave the room and she discovered that the doctor had come in. She walked his way and as she passed, she heard him say that he would keep her posted. Her only response was a nod of the head. She was not sure she could say anything yet.

She slowly walked to the elevator for trip three. The anger turned to sadness and then to despair. As the doors slid shut, she slowly sank to the floor. She recalled the feeling of falling and rising as the elevator transported visitors and staff. She had sat and cried with her knees up to her chest. Her arms squeezing her legs like she was squeeze the pain of his rejection away. She couldn't understand what had happened. All she knew is her husband didn't want her around. He didn't want anyone around.

She didn't know how long she had sat there. She had heard voices and saw legs move around her as people entered and left the elevator. A couple of nurses even knelt down to talk to her, but she barely noticed them. She finally pulled herself together enough that she could walk to her car. When she was in the safety of her vehicle, she cried out to God, "Why? Why God? Why is this happening? I don't understand! I don't know what to do! I don't know what comes next!" She sat there for a little bit longer before she felt like she had herself together enough to drive and made her way to his parents' house to get the kids.

Later, she walked into the home of Ryan's parents and was surprised to see Corp. Jones sitting on the couch with Tiffany. *Hmm when did that happen?* At least someone is having a normal life right now.

Tiffany had seen the curious look and whispered, "I'll tell ya later." With a nod that Emma had understood, she gathered his family around her and gave them all the news.

"How can they let him make a decision like that?" his mom asked with a hint of a whimper.

"He still has free will, Hannah. His body was injured, not his brain. But clearly he is not in a place to use it right now," stated Robert, his dad, shaking his head.

"Should we petition the court or something to get him to let us make the decisions since he is clearly not sane at the moment?" asked his brother, Mike.

"Mike, you know he isn't that far gone," Tiffany stated, in her sassy tone.

"We'll just pray for him. Not much we can do but follow his wishes, for now," remarked Robert, trying to be strong and hold it together. Everyone just sat in the living room in silence until it was broken by the cries of baby Sarah.

"I'll go get her," said Tiffany, as she jumped up from the couch. She stopped in front of Emma, "Anything you need, let me know. Cleaning, babysitting, you name it, I will be there. Free of charge." With a quick hug and a sniffle, she was up the stairs.

Help did come, daily. Her mom and dad came and stayed with her for a week or so, but had to head back home. Her dad had gotten a small maintenance job at a local RV park. When they left, Ryan's mother, sister and ladies from the church would come and check in on her and the kids. After a few more weeks, that stopped. The world kept moving when theirs had not. Ryan's sister, and Corp. Jones, still came by every other day to sit with the kids so Emma could go to the hospital to see if Ryan had changed his mind. It was all in vain. He still held firm to his choice.

Emma gradually moved passed some of the anger and was no longer calling him names in her head, but now she was just heartbroken and depressed. Her own doctor had even prescribed her some antidepressants to help get her through this. Some days it was all she could do to just change her clothes, let alone shower. She quit sleeping in their bed as it was too painful to lay next to where he should be. So she laid out a sleeping bag in Sarah's room and would sleep on the floor.

It had been the beginning of September when Ryan had his accident. One snowy Saturday afternoon in early December, Ann, one of Emma's closest friends, came to visit her. She was startled by the state of Emma's physical appearance as she answered the door.

"Emma girl, what have you done? Or not done I should ask. Where are the kids?" She glanced around the living room looking for the kids as she stepped in through the door and noticed it was quiet.

"Ryan's mom came and took them for a few days. I just couldn't do it. Aaron is fighting with me on everything. Stephen hasn't talked much since the accident. Sarah still doesn't like the formula. So, yeah..." She paused for a moment then let it go. "Ann? I don't know if I can keep doing this." Shaking her head and wobbling on her feet, Emma slouched over and Ann caught her as they both hit the floor. Emma began to sob, loudly. All Ann could do was silently pray as she held Emma. Not a single word was said.

After several minutes, Ann helped Emma up to the couch to sit.

"Emma? When was the last time you showered?"

"I don't know. Tuesday maybe."

"Girl that was 4 days ago. Come on. Let's go."

"I can't!"

"You must, you stink!" she said with a chuckle. "Let's get you cleaned up and dressed in some clean clothes and then we can figure the rest out."

Emma remembered being so weak that Ann had to guide her on the seat of the toilet while Ann started the shower for her and got clean clothes to wear. Ann was a hospice nurse, and Emma had watched as she went into nurse mode.

Ann came back into the bathroom, knelt in front of Emma and held her hands and looked searchingly at her.

"Emma, you know you can't keep going like this. You act like Ryan has died."

"He has, in a way. I mean he might as well have. Maybe this would have been easier." Emma paused and considered what she was about to tell her friend.

"On Monday, a man showed up at my door with divorce papers. Ann, I don't understand, why is he going to such …. extremes to push us, me away? Doesn't he know that when I said 'for better or worse' that I meant it? I just don't get it. Why would God do this to us?"

What her friend had said next changed how Emma had seen the situation. "God didn't do this to you, you know that. God spared Ryan's life. Things just happen. Human error is what happened here. God is with you and Ryan and your kids. Just don't lose sight of all you know in your heart. I don't know what makes a person decide to do the things they do, but we can only pray that God helps us through these times until we see the light at the end of the tunnel. Now let's get you in the tub and cleaned up. Get dressed and then you and I are going to go get some dinner. You have to keep moving forward, if nothing else, do it for the kids. They need you now more than ever. So let's go." From that day on, Emma thought of only what was best for the kids.

After lots of prayer and counseling with their pastor, she signed the divorce papers. She thought she was going to die as she did it. There were even water stains on them from her tears; tears of anger and sadness. She wanted to hit him and hug him all at the same moment but he wasn't there. He had promised to be there and he wasn't. Her emotions were all over the place and she hated it. She was a strong person, but she felt weak, helpless, and alone. Ryan had made sure that Emma and the kids were taken care of, at least for a little while. He had cashed out his 401K and made sure it was provided to her. Originally he had written in that she was to get all of the winnings of the lawsuit against the driver of the car that caused him to swerve to begin with. Emma had said no to that part of the agreement. Ryan needed something to live on.

Shortly after the divorce was complete, she had to make a hard choice – stay in the house they had bought and live penny to penny, or sell all they could and move in with her parents. She decided to sell. She was having a hard time living there without him anyway. She sent a message to Ryan through his lawyer of what she was doing and told him to let her know what he wanted but she never heard back. So she packed up most of his things and sent them to the thrift store. She kept a few mementos but for the most part she was still so angry that she was tired of looking at his things.

It had broken her heart to sell his motorcycle. They had shared so many memories on that bike, but he wasn't here to ride it and didn't send for it. So along with both cars, all their furniture, and all other housewares, she sold or gave things to friends in need. She sold the house and moved across state to live with her parents.

She hated doing it. They had married right out of high school and she only had worked part-time until she became pregnant with Stephen. Without having much work experience or a degree in anything, she knew if she didn't move in with them all the money would be gone quickly. Thankfully, her parents' house had plenty of space for them. By Valentine's Day, they were moved and settled in.

It was hard to have to sleep in a room with her children, but it was better than sleeping in a big bed next to where he had once slept. The boys slept on the floor or in bed with her. Sarah slept in an old port-a-crib at the foot of the bed. It was a comfort to have them so close at night. It was as if the kids knew they needed each other. There was a feeling of comfort and a resemblance of peace returned to what was left of their family.

After giving the kids a month to settle in at mom and dad's, she had to do something for an income. She got a job at the local superstore. The pay wasn't the greatest but it had insurance, so it was enough. She knew she needed something more than just a job though. So at the age of twenty-five, when her high school classmates were graduating college, she was enrolling into college. She would major in Secondary Education with minors in History and World Cultures.

A loud, blistering ring of a school bell brought her back to the present. Things had been difficult but the rewards made it better.

She put on a big smile as her classroom filled with students. It was the first day of the new school year and a new life for her and the kids. Change was in the air.

"Good morning freshman!   Welcome to World History!"

Chapter 2

He couldn't believe it had been eight years. Eight long, agonizing, foolish years. He knew now that he could have stayed, but he had been crazy enough to think otherwise.

He pummeled another nail into the wall of his home; a home that had been a gift. It was an unused property that gave him the seclusion and privacy he needed and desired. It was out of town and away from people. The owner had agreed to let him live in the home if he maintained the property. The old woman had no one to care for the house and acreage and he was willing to help her out with the repairs it needed. She didn't realize that she was helping him get back on his feet after years of neglect to himself.

One more nail driven into the wall as images of where he once was came back to mind.

He left the hospital on a rainy day with a cane in his hand and a limp in his walk. He insisted that his lawyer bring him some clothes and all his money that was being held for him until he could get out. He wanted his Harley, but he had received a letter from her the day before he checked himself out that she sold it along with everything else. That Harley was his release. He could always clear his head when he was on his bike. Now he would have to leave this town.

When the lawyer came with what he asked for, he had walked out of the hospital and went straight to the bar. He had never been a drinker but he figured he had nothing to lose. Everything was gone now, so why not finish the job. After closing down the bar, he staggered right out of town. With his heavy camouflage coat, pockets full of his medications and cash, he was shaking this town off like the dirt he felt like. He didn't care that his parents would be heartbroken and he sure didn't care if she was hurting or not. She signed on the dotted line. He promised himself to push his family out of his mind and heart, and when he was drunk and had taken his pain medications, it wasn't hard to do. When the medication was gone he didn't get a refill.

He settled in the first city he came to and that's where he stayed for the first year. It wasn't hard to find a small apartment. He had nothing. He wanted nothing. He was content living on macaroni and cheese, eggs and cheap beer. Unfortunately, you cannot live on bread alone. He had to find a job. The one time he went out into the businesses with his resume, he frightened a poor woman conducting the interviews. He told himself he would never let that happen again. So he stayed inside all day and went out at night. He found a job working as the janitor at an office building. They didn't care how he looked and he would be cleaning after hours. After his shift, he spent every night at the local bars. Drinking her away. Drinking them away. After almost a year of separation from his family, he was becoming desperate to forget them. He couldn't hide from the images of his family back home. He knew in his heart that it was God telling him to go home, but his head told him not to. He kept telling himself he was too great a burden for Emma.

One day, he had a knock on his door. In yet another hung-over state, he answered. He was startled by who it was. He worried they had found him. It was Pastor Cross. He wondered if the man recognized him. The look on the man of God's face told him otherwise. He hadn't shaved since the day he walked out of the hospital and he didn't remember showering in a couple days. He thought he even noticed a bit of the recoil that he had seen on every face he walked by. He didn't invite the pastor in, but he was sure he had been rude to the man. Their words were few, but what Pastor Cross said to him that day stayed with him for the next few years.

"Son, I don't know you from the next guy, but I can see you are in need. Just know, running from God and those who love you doesn't get you very far. Here is my card and if you ever want to talk, feel free to come by the church, and we will talk."

With a nod and a handshake, the man was gone and he decided to leave town the next day. He was not going to risk it anymore.

He drifted the country for six years. Until one night in Georgia, while he was walking home from a night at the bar, he saw a big white tent peeking over the tops of the trees. The closer he got to the tent, the louder the music became.

Singing, a piano, drums, a tambourine, a guitar, all playing together in a beautiful tune. One he had not heard in many years. He came closer yet and he heard a few shouts and whoops of joy and excitement. He had to see what was happening. It just seemed to draw him in. He felt like a thirsty camel in the middle of a desert. It was an oasis to him.

Standing just outside of the tent peering in, he realized it was a tent revival. He had an old familiar feeling start to take form in the pit of his stomach. He felt a need to respond to what he was seeing. He had been to many of these in his younger years. He had come to know Jesus Christ as his Lord and Savior at an old tent revival.

The loud and expressive minister reminded him of his pastor back home. A man he liked and admired. He stepped through the threshold of that tent, and walked right to the front and sat down in the chair the minister just got out of. He didn't care what the congregation thought about his smell or appearance. He had an old need to hear what this man had to say. As the man preached, he knew that this night things were about to change. Sure enough, twenty minutes into the message, he found himself kneeling on the ground right in front of the man of God, seeking forgiveness from God. When all was said and done, he decided that he was done running.

He told the minister after the service, all that he had been running from and what happened. By the time he was finished, he was sobbing so hard that he could no longer talk. The minister wrapped an arm over his shoulders and said these words, "God is into giving second chances. You have walked away from Him and your family and you have seen how wrong it was. Now that you have chosen to let God have control again. It is time for you to go home."

Through tear stained sobs, his response to the minister was, "What if she isn't there?"

"Why don't you let God make things happen in her and just do your part?" After a bit of a pause, he asked, "Do you need a ride son?" He had declined but still did as the minister had told him.

The night he reached his home town, a local police officer found him sitting by the side of the road. He was at war with himself. He wanted to go into town and find Pastor Cross but at the same time, he wanted to run the other way. He kept telling himself that God made him a new person and he didn't need to run anymore.

Unfortunately, the officer thought he was drunk and because he didn't respond to the questioning they took him downtown to the station. While emptying his pockets, one kind officer offered him the business card of his pastor, so he called the man and asked him to come down. Pastor Cross took him home, cleaned him up, counseled him, and made sure to find him jobs around the town. In one of their weekly meetings six months ago, he finally told the pastor who he really was. The man told him he already knew his identity and was excited to have him home again.

The ring of his cell phone brought him echoed through the empty room. He had been mindlessly nailing away at the drywall and was surprised he didn't do any damage. The phone rang again and he reached into his pocket to retrieve it.

The name on the caller ID said *Pastor*, so he willingly answered.

"Hey there, Pastor. What can I do for ya?"

"You can meet me at Tony's to celebrate."

"Sure. Not sure what we are celebrating, but I could use some food. What time?"

"Meet me there at 5:30. This old man needs to be in bed by 8."

They laughed in unison as he promised to meet his pastor and friend at the pizza joint.

Chapter 3

After a long first day at a new school, all Emma wanted to do was go home and take a long soak in her beautiful claw-foot tub. Instead, as she unlocked the door to their new house where she was met with stacks of boxes.

"Grandpa and Uncle Dan have been here!" exclaimed Stephen as he walked in behind her.

"I thought for sure we had less stuff than this," chimed in Aaron.

"You think they put boxes in the right rooms?" asked Sarah.

"Honey, it looks like it was all just put in the living room and dining room. You have two strong brothers to help move things around," replied Emma as she gave her sweet baby girl a side hug and smacked Stephen on the back.

She had accepted the teaching position at her old high school and signed on the house a week ago. It had been a crazy month. After four years of college and three years of teaching in some elementary school miles away in Toledo, she had finally found her way back home. Back to small town living and was blessed to find the position at her alma- mater available. She was not a big city girl by any means. The traffic and noise was enough to make this small town girl go nuts. And the men, well, just don't even get her started on them. She had tried her hand at dating a couple of times, but it never felt right. She always walked in with a pit in her stomach the size of Texas. She walked out of the date singing the Hallelujah Chorus as she shook off yet another guy. That said something in her book. The last guy tried to be "dad" to the kids right off the bat and that didn't sit well with any of them, so he was the last straw.

That was a year ago.

They had lived in an apartment all of the last four years and she was ready for wide open spaces and fresh air. She was a little uneasy about coming back home and seeing old friends and family. She couldn't avoid it though. It was like God shut every door but this one. With all the applications and resumes she put out there, this was the only one that did not fall through. God was clearly telling her this is where she belonged. She was ready for the change. Ready to get back to her roots. Ready to come home.

Her hometown didn't have anything exciting or unusual. No rolling hills or great fishing holes. No massive manufacturing plants that employ more than half the town. It just had a lot of farmland and a few curvy roads that were fun to drive on. It was basic but it was her hometown. The place where she and the kids were born. The place where she met Ryan. The place where her favorite church and pastor were. Her best and favorite memories were here. A lot had changed in the eight years since she had left here.

The town had added some new chain stores and restaurants. Downtown and Main Street had gotten a face lift. She also had no family support here. Her parents still lived on the other side of the state and Ryan's parents moved out of the state two years after the accident. They held on as long as they could in hopes that Ryan would come around. They had heard that after he was done with therapy, treatments and couple of surgeries, he checked himself out of the hospital and disappeared. There were rumors that he had been seen around town in different bars but then the rumors stopped and nothing was heard of him again. He clearly had wanted nothing to do with anyone who knew him and loved him. So they moved on as well. She still kept in touch with her in-laws and made trips to visit them, but it wasn't like it was before. The closeness wasn't there as much, except with Tiffany. She had become a godsend even after they moved.

Whenever she could, Tiffany would make a trip to visit Emma and the kids for at least a day or two before she went to see her parents. Although she was much younger than Emma, they had become close friends. After about a year of her and Corp. Jones dating, he asked her to marry him. That was an odd moment for Emma. To stand next to Ryan's sister as matron of honor as she married the man who had saved Ryan's life. Emma thought he was a good guy and welcomed him openly, but it never felt right not having Ryan there. She knew Tiffany had been hurt by it.

The transition from Toledo to here was smooth. Emma felt blessed by all that God had worked out to get her here. She didn't understand why He wanted her here, but she was not about to tell Him "No". He had provided a home and a job and she gave Him a willing heart.

The house was on eight acres of land. The Peterson's had given her a great deal. The old couple were ready to move closer to town and closer to their children and grandchildren. She really felt like she paid too little for the place. She had quite a savings set aside to be able to almost pay for the house in full, but they were insistent on the price. Mrs. Peterson even got on her about not "knocking a gift horse in the mouth" and that God wanted them to do this and they were good with that.

"What would we do with that much money anyway?" She knew they were just being overly nice. Old Mr. Peterson told her.

"Just take it honey. Your kids need these wide open spaces. To make you feel better, I insist that you allow me and my boys to continue to hunt and fish here, for life. But if at any point you want to sell the place, please let us know first. I would like to see it back in the family if at all possible." She could agree with that, so she did as she was told. It truly was a beautiful place.

Six acres were wooded. Right now the property was in all its glory as the colors were beginning to change. It had been a cooler than normal summer, so it seemed like fall was coming early. Emma was excited to watch the change happen. In the middle of this wooded area was a large pond that was going to be great for some fishing and summer swimming. Mr.

Peterson said it was fully stocked with all kinds of fish. There was a path that led from the back porch to the pond. Nothing major to take away from the ambiance of the property, but enough that you could easily find your way there and back. She felt such peace out here and the thought of having uncut woods behind and beside her brought out the excitement of her inner treasure hunter. The rest was lush, green yard space. Her boys were going to love her when it came time to mow this yard though. All they owned was a good old push mower. She would get a riding mower, eventually.

The house was a large, brick farmhouse with deep blue shutters that flanked each window and white trim. When she first saw the house, the color combination of red, white, and blue did not go unnoticed and it made her smile. The porch and a swing that graced the front of the house gave an inviting feeling to anyone who climbed the steps. She could imagine herself entertaining her friends, the few left in town, with good conversation and a good cup of coffee. This is what sold her on this house, that and the claw-foot tub she was still longing for at this moment.

When you walked through the front door, you found yourself in the living room. The hardwood floors and wood trim were bare and in good shape. They had that fresh look about them. She hoped that the Peterson's had not refinished them just for her. To the left of the living room was another room that was used as an office. This made a great space for her to put a desk to do her school work. There was a doorway that flowed right into the kitchen. The kitchen was amazing. A large apron sink sat right beneath another large window that overlooked the backyard and into the woods. She also had a double oven, which Sarah loved because she was the resident baker. In the middle of the rather large kitchen was an island that held a cook-top. She would welcome the large cooking and prep space come the holidays. The downstairs bathroom and the laundry room were off the kitchen on one side. Through a large doorway that pointed you back in the direction of the front of the house was the dining area which then flowed right in to the living room again. The stairs to the second floor were between the living room and dining room. She could see Aaron and Sarah chasing each other through all the doorways around the stairs. It would be like a race track.

The kids' bathroom was just off the kitchen. Upstairs had four bedrooms and a bathroom. The master bedroom and bathroom overlooked the backyard. The other rooms flanked the staircase on each side with an open space in the middle that had built-in bookshelf and a desk-like area which would work great for one of the kids to do their schoolwork. All throughout the house was the original trim and beautiful hardwood floors.

There was one space in the house though that Emma knew would become her personal sanctuary. The room was just off the back side of the kitchen. Through a heavy door that would shut out noise in the rest of the house, was a screened in porch. They called it a Michigan room. It was three walls covered in windows and it had an electric fireplace. Emma could see her chaise lounge and lamp by the windows and all her bookshelves would go on the wall that clearly at one time was the backside of the house. This would be her place of refuge from preteen boys and an increasingly emotional little girl. She loved her kids and couldn't imagine her life without them, but every mother knows, she needed a place like this in her home. It would be her space. No Kids Allowed!

"Hey Ma! What are we going to have for dinner? There's no food yet." Leave it to Stephen to state the obvious.

"See the woods out back, get your gun and have at it Bud!" she jokingly replied.

"Yeah, okay mom, I am right on that." Stephen said with all the attitude he had as he stomped up the stairs to check out his room.

"Hey! You could at least take a box up with you!" she yelled up the stairs after him. The response was a slammed door. She could tell that his tween and teen years could be the death of her.

"Boy, he sure is grumpy tonight," commented Sarah.

"Yeah, he has been all day. I think he misses the old school." Aaron said.

Stephen, who was now twelve and starting his seventh grade year, was always either really mellow or really moody. There wasn't much of an in-between.

When Ryan disappeared, Stephen started to withdraw from people. He spent a lot of his time in his room or fighting with his brother. As he got older, he shut out the real world with video games. No matter how many times she tried, she couldn't break the cycle. Emma hated that he was missing out on a childhood. He walked around with the weight of the world on his little shoulders. Well, now his big shoulders. He was growing into a handsome young man. If the youth pastor of their former church had not stepped in, she knew Stephen would be worse off than he is now. But you just can't contend with hormones. Yes, she was very proud of her "Lil'Man". There were many times recently that Emma had to do a double take because his physical features were beginning to resemble Ryan.

Aaron, on the other hand, who was now ten, was the one child in the family who was going to do it his way, no matter what anyone said. He had been since the day he was born, but it intensified after the accident. It was like once he realized daddy was not coming home, he acted out constantly. She had read all the books she could find, talked to all the moms she had met, and even brought the pastor in for a "talking to" and it never changed. She figured she would do the best she could and follow God's leading with this one. She prayed morning and night for him, for all three of her children, but she spent a couple extra minutes on him. He worried her sometimes. He was a very good looking kid, and he knew it. She knew he didn't get the cockiness genetically from his dad, who was awkward and shy. Maybe it came from her side of the family. All the men are pretty confident in themselves. Emma, let out a little snicker at the thought.

Sarah looked at her mom, "What's so funny mom?"

"Nothing baby, just thinking."

Sarah, her sweet baby girl. She was a beauty as a baby, with her heart shaped lips and button nose, and she was a beauty at eight. Emma could not imagine her life without her dad, and her baby girl had gone her whole life without hers. Sarah would never know what it was like to be "daddy's girl" and it hurt Emma's heart. She tried to not think on all that was lost because of what Ryan forced them to go through. If she did, she would not be able to move. The bitterness would consume her.

"Let's go to the pizza parlor downtown. Come on, Stephen! Let's go!" she yelled up the stairs at him. With the thunder of size ten feet, he ran down the stairs and out the door. He was already taller than her and she hated it.

Everyone climbed into the red SUV and they made their way into town. From the back, she could hear music blaring out of Aaron's headphones. She had Sarah tap him on the shoulder to get him to turn it off and join the family for a while. With a heavy sigh, he did as he was told. Wow! Wonders never cease! He did as he was told. Thank you God!

"Hey Mom, you aren't going to cry or anything while you drag us down 'memory lane' are you? If so, turn around and leave me home." There is the Aaron I know and love.

"I promise to try not to, Bud" she replied. She mentally scolded herself for letting the children see how emotional she felt. *Keep yourself together Emma. They need you to be strong.*

***

Stephen knew his mom tried to hide her emotions from him and his brother and sister. He didn't know if the other two had caught it as well, but he could tell his mom was about to crack.

He heard her cry from his room while she was getting a shower this morning. He didn't understand why and it made him sad that his mom seemed unhappy.

Maybe moving here wasn't a good idea after all.

Chapter 4

As they parked the vehicle and climbed out, Emma paused at the curb. She was frozen in time just by the sight of the old pizzeria. She could not believe how much it had not changed. Same red, green and white colors. Same wood sign with beautiful scroll work that stated this was "Tony's Pizzeria". From what she could see, it even had the same vinyl booth covers inside. It was like time stopped in there and she hoped she could keep her promise to the kids on the way here.

Tony's was the gathering place of all teenagers in this town back when she and Ryan were in high school. There were many dates here between the two of them. She had not had an emotional response when she thought about her days with Ryan in a long time, but she could feel her throat tighten up, her nose stuff up, and water begin to pool in the inner corners of her eyes. This was not going to be as easy as she thought. God! I need you to help me through this. I am not sure I can right now.

As they walked in the door, they were greeted by a young girl, maybe seventeen, who with a false smile, offered to seat them.

"Table or booth?"

"Booth, please."

The restaurant was busy and she recognized a few faces. An old friend, the one who pulled her out of her misery all those years ago, Ann, came over to her and gave her a hug that was so tight yet so warm that it felt like a blanket of comfort wrapped around her shoulders. They stood there in an embrace for several moments.

"I didn't know you were in town. I have missed you," Ann told her.

"Yeah, we just moved back."

"You're not here to visit? You're here to stay?" she said with almost a shout.

"Yup! I am the new history teacher at the high school. Signed on the Peterson place last week and dad and Dan moved the boxes in today."

"Why didn't you call me and tell me? I would have had a meal ready and waiting or at least come to greet you."

"We wanted it to be a surprise to everyone but mom and dad and Dan." She gave a sheepish grin, "Sorry. We are home now and you and I have some catching up to do."

"Yes we do! Your cell number still the same?"

"Sure is, call me tomorrow and we will work it out."

"Ma'am, your table is right this way," interrupted the waitress.

"Sorry. See you later Ann," she said as she followed the young lady to their table.

On the way to the table, she noticed that her beloved pastor and friend was there as well and he seemed to be visiting with a man who clearly did not want to be noticed and was very uncomfortable in such a bustling, public place. He sat slouched over the checkered tablecloth with the hood of his shirt over his head. She barely caught a glimpse of his face, but what she did see caused her to pause. Massive scars on his face that traveled down his neck and disappeared into his shirt collar. She could only guess that they didn't stop at his neck. Something about him did seem familiar to her though. *I wonder...no that's not possible.*

***

He didn't want to be here. Pastor Cross had thought it would be a good idea to celebrate his year of sobriety and the anniversary of his return to town after years of running. Running from her and from God.

This meeting was supposed to be a relaxing night. A guy's night out. When he saw the people he had been running from for the last eight years walk in, he wanted to bolt for the back door.

"What is she doing here?" he whispered with angst as he watched his past walk in the door. A past that he hated himself for, he knew he was a fool for doing it. He was not prepared for this. He was not ready to see her again. If he was honest with himself, he was not ready for her to see him. "Pastor, I can't stay. Thanks for dinner, but I can't," he told the man across the table from him.

"Why not, David? What's wrong? Do you feel alright? You just turned three shades of white." David was the name he had given people.

He didn't hear the pastor's questions because he was too entranced by his thoughts of running again. When he did glance at her, she amazed him. She walked with confidence and strength. Everyone looked fairly happy. She looked happy. He knew she was capable of raising the kids without him and everyone seemed to be fine. The last thing he wanted though was for them to see him.

"Why didn't you tell me they had moved back into town? I can't see her or run into her or...man the kids are getting big." His heart stopped at the thought of all he has missed out on. *My daughter is so big. Where did the baby go? Has it really been that long?*

"I would say that was a safe guess. Honestly, I didn't realize she had moved back. I had not heard anything about it. She looks good, David. It looks like she has found a good life." He turned to look at David and was met with the scariest glare he had ever had shot his way. "What?"

"She looks good! That's all you can say? What kind of pastor are you? No words of wisdom to help me deal with this? Just a comment on how good she looks?" He could feel the panic in his chest. His heart was racing and it was getting hard to breathe.

"David, you know what you should do. You just chose not to do it. God has just thrown your family back in your lap, now what are you going to do?"

David didn't respond, he just watched as his former family made their way in his direction. The movements played in his mind in slow motion. His palms began to sweat as she looked right at him. His stomach dropped to the floor. *I make her sick. I can see it. Oh I'm not ready for this. Please don't sit nearby! God, she is still so beautiful.* He closed his eyes and bowed his head for a moment, like he was praying for his meal, and then he heard her.

"Pastor Cross! Oh my goodness, it is so good to see you." She leaned down to hug the pastor who had been a friend to them, married them and did each of their children's dedications. "Are you still pastor at Cornerstone? Please tell me you are, because I'm eager to hear your sermons again."

"I sure am. They can't get rid of me until the Father calls me Home. Are you home visiting?"

"No we are here to stay," she answered.

"Are these your kids? Wow! How they have grown. You don't have kids anymore, you have young men and a beautiful young lady."

"I sure do. No more babies Pastor, they have all grown up on me. Kids, say hi to Pastor Cross."

The boys said hi, but David could feel a pair of eyes on him and it made his skin crawl. He glanced to his right out of the corner of his eye and saw his daughter staring at him, except he didn't see fear in her sweet eyes, only compassion and confusion.

"Oh where are my manners? This is David. He is, um, somewhat new in the area." Pastor looked at David. grinning like the cat that got the mouse.

"Hello" he said very sternly.

"Um, hi. Nice to meet you, David. How long have you been in the area?"

Do I have to do this? He chose not to respond.

"How long have you been gone now?" Pastor asked taking attention away from him.

"Well, last we lived here was about seven years ago. Remember? I left right after, well you know." He could tell she didn't want to talk about it.

He glanced at her left hand while they talked. He noticed that there was no ring on her left hand, not even a tan line. Guilt washed over him

"Well, um, I will leave you gentlemen to your meal. The kids are getting hungry. It was nice to meet you David. Pastor Cross, we will see you Sunday."

"That will be wonderful. It is good to have you back in town" Pastor Cross replied. They moved to the booth behind David and sat down.

"Now that wasn't so bad, was it?" the pastor asked him in a hushed tone and a sly grin on his face.

"I thought I was going to die. My nerves had me shaking so bad. Man! Don't do that to me again."

"Well David, she and the kids will be in church on Sunday, so be ready to see them again."

"Maybe it is time to find a new church," David said with a little snicker.

"Mommy, what do you think happened to that man?" he heard his little girl ask her mother. Her voice sounded so sweet and innocent. Now all he wanted to do was cry. He put his elbows on the table and put his head in his hands. He could feel the pressure of the tears forming on the back of his eyes. He could hear everything they said, and as much as he wanted to run, he wanted to be sitting right there with them, to be as near to them, to her, as he could. But he made his choice eight years ago and he saw no way of changing that.

"I am not sure honey, it looks like it was bad, whatever it was. Oh sweetie, don't cry about it. Pray for him."

He heard a small sniffle. "But Mom, to suffer that much..." She had such a tender heart.

He wanted to go but he could not pull away yet. He couldn't leave his family yet.

It had been years since he was this close to his kids and he missed her so much. She had a gentle touch that warmed him every time. She had a way to make his blood boil when she looked at him. He knew how she felt about him with just a look. She was so precious to him. *So why'd you do it you ding-dong? You know it wouldn't have changed the way you felt about each other.* He wasn't willing to take that risk or to put the weight of his treatments and therapies on her. He hated himself for being so distracted by his thoughts that he couldn't respond to the oncoming car like he should have. He also hated himself for letting such a gem go.

You're a fool Daniels!

Pastor Cross sat and watched David as they listened to the conversations go on behind him.

Some of it was funny. Aaron was a class clown but very arrogant. "Hope that doesn't get him in too much trouble" he said to Pastor. Stephen didn't seem to say much, just like himself - strong and silent.

Then he heard one of the boys say, "Mom, think you will ever marry again?" David didn't want to know her answer.

"I can't do this Pastor. I'll talk to you later." He tossed some ones on the table for a tip and stormed for the door. What did you expect, for her to become a nun and the kids to stay little?

He hated how he let the accident kill his family.

***

Stephen watched the scarred man walk out of the pizzeria. He couldn't help it. There was just something about him that made Stephen feel like he knew the man who was walking out the door with his carved, wooden cane. He could see all the scarring on the right side of his face, but when all he could see was the man's left side, he could have sworn it was his dad. He sat there as he watched the man leave, trying to remember what his dad looked like. He had a feeling his dad looked a lot like this man.

Chapter 5

"Stephen, let's not talk about this here. You know I am not even willing to think about it. Not right now." Emma was shocked that he would bring it up. She could feel her face turning red from embarrassment. This was too personal of a topic to discuss with her son.

Stephen, with his stinker smile stretched across his face proceeded to say, "Mom, what's the big deal? Are you just nervous about getting back in the …"

"That is enough, Honey. We can talk about this later if you want to." How he managed to go from brooding tween to a joker within minutes surprised her sometimes.

"Here's your pizza!" exclaimed the young waitress. The girl had pink hair and various piercings. As she set the tray down, Emma noticed that Aaron was watching the girl with the silly school boy grin Ryan used to give her. *Oh dear Lord, I am less ready for this than I am dating again!*

On the trip home, Stephen asked, "Mom, can we really have that talk when we get home? I wasn't trying to embarrass you. I guess it was a bad place to bring it up, but there was a reason."

"Okay Bud, but let's get stuff in the house first. Give me twenty minutes and meet me on the swing."

"K"

When they arrived back home, everyone carried boxes to their rooms so that they could find their things the next day. Emma wanted her children to get back into a routine as fast as possible. Her dad and brother had brought furniture up to the rooms and put beds together and dressers in place. Emma was glad that all she really had to do was put sheets on the bed and climb in, but first, she had to find her comfy black yoga pants and her old band t-shirt, well, Ryan's t-shirt. It was faded and you really couldn't see the letters very well, but the memory of that first date was forever in her heart.

He'd picked her up in his 79 Malibu. She couldn't tell if it just had a loud muffler or a big engine. It wasn't the prettiest shade of green either. In fact, it kind of made her think of something she saw when she changed baby diapers while babysitting. It really didn't matter. He had finally asked her on a date and she was excited. They had been flirting and passing notes for two months and she was getting a little tired of the game. She knew in her heart he was the one for her. So what if they were only in high school. If you let God work things out, anything is possible.

He came to the door and instead of being met by her, he came face to face with her dad, Tom, "Big Tom" as some people in town called him. She was standing at the top of the stairs watching the face off and felt sorry for Ryan as he didn't stand a chance against her dad. Dad was a retired Marine and did not mess around when it came to his baby girl.

"What do you want, boy?" she heard her dad say.

"Um, I am here to take your daughter to a concert, sir."

"What kind of concert?" He gave the band name. "Well, who are they?"

"A Christian group, sir. Uh, DCTalk, sir."

"Never heard of them. Who all is going? Emma can't date yet."

"The youth group I am part of, sir."

"Tom, leave the poor boy alone! Emma! Your friend is here!" her mom yelled. Her voice held a hint of humor and compassion for Ryan. Emma figured it was time to come down anyway. Ryan had been tortured enough.

"Coming mama! Hi Ryan! Mom, Dad, this is Ryan."

"Ryan, this is Tom and Evelyn Edwards."

"Mr. and Mrs. Edwards to you, Ryan." Her dad said his name like it was sour milk. Emma just kept her giggle to herself. Her dad and Ryan were handling this meeting superficially well.

"Dad, he is safe. Don't worry. He is just a friend." *For now.*

"Tom, ease up dear, you knew the day was coming that the boys would start knocking on our door. Come help me in the kitchen so these two can get going. Will you be home by 11? Emma?"

Emma looked at Ryan for the answer.

"Yeah". There was a slight squeak of horror in his voice. "Yes, I should have her home by then. If it lasts any longer than 10:30, we will leave early," Ryan told her parents.

"Alright, well you kids have a good time," her mom said as she pushed them out the door.

"I thought your dad was going to hit me and throw me to the curb, literally throw me," Ryan stated.

"Don't let him worry you too much. He may act tough and mean, but really, he will give you the shirt off his back if you need it. You will see the more you get to know each other." Emma gave him a reassuring smile and got in the car.

"MOM! WHERE'S MY MP3 PLAYER?" Aaron yelled from his room at the front of the house, waking her from her walk down memory lane. She put the shirt on and walked to his room.

"Did you bring it in from the truck?"

"Um, I don't think so!"

"Well then, dear, go get it." She patted him on the cheek and walked down to the kitchen to start unpacking boxes.

This day felt like it was never going to end. She was so tired and emotionally drained that she found it hard to think and walk at the same time. To prove her point, at that moment she found herself falling face first into a stack of boxes. She tripped over a flat spot on the floor. There was nothing around to trip on, but plenty to fall into. She tried to catch herself before she knocked boxes over, but failed completely as she took down five boxes. She knew the contents of at least one of said boxes suffered worse than she did as she heard glass break. Next was a thunder of footsteps coming at her from upstairs.

"Mom! You okay?" Sarah asked.

"I'm fine. A bit of a klutz but fine. Not so sure about whatever is in these boxes though."

"It was all our cups ma," Aaron stated with a hint of irritation reflected in his voice. Stephen helped Emma up as Aaron moved boxes and opened them. "They are all in pieces."

"Good thing we have disposable ones somewhere," Stephen said.

"You know what, just leave it for now. Clearly I am not in any shape to unpack, so I am going to go sit on the swing out front. You guys go ahead and get ready for bed. It has been a long day."

"Mom, our talk?" Stephen reminded her.

"Right, swing. Sarah! Aaron! Bed! Now! Let's go Honey."

As she walked out the door, she heard Sarah ask, "What is going on with her? She is acting funny."

Aaron answered, "Today is the anniversary of dad's accident."

"Oh!"

"I can't believe it has been eight years," stated Aaron.

"I wish I had met him," commented Sarah.

"Come on, let's go. I don't want to get in trouble," she heard Aaron say followed by footsteps fading up the stairs.

It was peaceful out here, with the sound of bullfrogs communicating, crickets chirping and the wind blowing. A woman could easily lose herself out here. She sat on the swing next to Stephen and enjoyed the gentle sway of it as she tried to clear her head so she could give him all her attention. She failed though. Just as soon as she righted her mind and took a deep breath to relax, the face of the stranger she met flashed in her memory. She could not get past how familiar the man with Pastor Cross seemed to her.

What was his name again? That's right, David. David, hmmm.

He had seemed so closed off and in a panic that she didn't dare ask any questions. Not like it was any of her business. The fact that she felt like she knew him began to nag at her. Was it his temperament or the way he looked at her? One side of his face was all scarred and mangled, almost like he had been mauled by a bear or in a terrible fire. The other side had a few scars and marks, but not half as bad as the other. Her heart hurt for the stranger and she decided to put him into her prayers tonight. Everyone needs someone praying for them.

"Mom? You okay?" she heard Stephen ask, bringing her back to the porch swing, sitting next to her son.

"Yeah, I am good," she gave him a fake smile, "just a lot on my mind."

"We can talk another time if you want," He said as he started to get up.

"No, No, No! I told you we would chat. What's on your mind?"

"So the guy sitting with the pastor..."

"Yeah, Pastor Cross and David."

"Did he remind you of any one?"

"Well, he seems familiar but I can't figure out who. Why do you ask?"

"He kind of made me think of, well, of dad. But that can't be because dad isn't around here. Is he? I mean if he was, wouldn't he come looking for us?"

"Oh, Honey, I don't know. That accident changed him more than we thought. The man I sent off to work that day would not have done this." *At least I don't think he would have. Maybe I didn't know your daddy as well as I thought I did.*

"I asked God every day to bring him back to us. I really didn't care how he looked, I just wanted him back in our lives. I wanted to take care of him and help nurse him back to normal but..." she had to stop before she said too much more. She did not want to burden her son with her emotional drama.

"It's okay mom, I can handle it. But what?"

"I don't want to burden you with my insecurities Stephen. You already take on too much. You missed out on being a kid so far. I don't want that for you."

She heard a heavy sigh coming from her son. He wanted to fix everything, and she could see it, but this was her fight.

"Okay. Well can I ask why you never married again?"

"I don't know honey. I guess I just never found the right guy. None of them were," she paused to think. *How do I say this?*

"Dad?"

She reflected on the emotion and intuition she had with each date. She then realized her son had figured her out better that she could figure herself out.

"You're right, they weren't your dad. But also, nothing ever seemed right. I never felt that jolt of excitement with the handful of guys I did go out with. If there is no spark, it isn't worth it to me. Maybe I am not supposed to marry. I had my time and I was happy. Maybe. Well, oh hon, I really do not know." She could feel her eyes fill with tears and she looked down to her hand in her lap.

Another hand joined hers, "It's okay mom. I don't expect you to know it all. Well, I'll see ya in the morning." He leaned over and kissed her on the cheek, "Night Mama."

"Night Baby."

She followed him inside and grabbed her iPod. She knew where hers was. She found the docking station, plugged it all in and pointed the player out the window so she could listen to some music and relax a bit. The first song to play on her play list was a country song sung by a married couple. In the song, the chorus was saying that this life would kill them if they didn't have the other person. Emma gave a little huff and said out loud, "It won't kill you, but you will wish it had." She turned it off, locked up the house and headed for bed. She was done with the day and all the emotions that went with it.

Good night cruel world.

Chapter 6

Two weeks had gone by and everyone seemed fairly settled in. Rooms were set up and already a mess with laundry all over the floors. Emma's room on the other hand was still full of boxes yet to unpack. She had the basics out, but that was it. She needed a day or two to get herself settled. Trying to get kids settled, grade papers, and put the house together was proving to be a greater task than she thought she could handle. She just wanted the unpacking fairy to come and finish everything up for her. She was ready to get back to normal and have everything in place and was tired of digging for everything.

Now every mother knows, with changes come arguments. The kids seemed like they had been fighting nonstop since they moved in. It was just silly things like, "Mom, he's touching me!" or "he is on my side of the room!" There was an inner need to have peace and quiet again. She needed a break from all of it, desperately.

As she sat there in on the porch swing with her coffee in one hand and Bible in her lap, she looked out at the field across the road from her.

The corn was still high, but starting to brown from the cold. On the back side of the field was the woods. All the trees were in full color. Reds, burgundies, oranges and yellows, and a few greens as well. It was beautiful. Stephen had taken a picture of the view the day before. Emma had a feeling he was looking for the same serenity she was. She had heard fall blow in a week ago on the back of streamline winds. Today, when it was a cool, sunny morning, she could smell it. She loved this time of year.

As she sat there and enjoyed the sway of her swing, she thought on all she wanted to get done today. Off in her own little world, she heard someone coming down the dirt road. She watched her parents' SUV pull in the driveway. Surprised, she got up and she met her mom half way between the house and driveway.

"Hi mom! This is a surprise! Come on in!" She waved at her dad as they headed for the house.

"Your dad and I thought we would come and get the kids and take them for a couple days. You have been here two weeks and we haven't seen them since the day you moved in. We know you are busy, but I want to have my grandbabies over."

"Mom, you do know they are not babies anymore, right?"

"They still are to me, just like you are," she said as she patted Emma on her face. "Now where are they?"

"Up in their rooms still. We just had breakfast."

"I'll go get them, you sit and enjoy your cup of coffee."

Instead of having a seat on the swing, she turned and went out to say hi to her dad. She wanted to make sure she had thanked him for the help with the move.

"Didn't feel like coming in and saying hi?"

"My knees have been bugging me, so the less climbing and walking I do the better."

"You up for having the kids around?"

"Well of course. I am going to put those boys to work getting the house ready for winter. They are calling for a cold one this year. You ready?"

"I think so but I will let you double check the house when you feel up to it. By the way, if I didn't say so before, thank you for all your help with the move and getting settled in. I really appreciate it."

"Anytime, Pumpkin." He patted her hand and smiled at her. *He looks so tired.* Her thought was interrupted with the sound of Sarah yelling "Hi" to her papa and the heavy front door shutting with a rather loud thud.

They both looked toward the house to see her mom and the kids make their way to the car. "You cool with being here by yourself, mom?" asked Stephen.

"I will be fine Stephen. I am a grown woman and the mother of three crazy kids. Go have fun." She kissed each of the kids as they climbed into the car and she stood on the porch steps and waved until they turned onto the main road. *Silence at last! Time for me' time. Now what do I do? Do I do some house cleaning or go for a walk?*

Her inner explorer won the struggle, a walk in the woods it is. She knew that she really needed to unpack, but she was also eager to explore her property some more, to go beyond the two acres of yard. She hadn't taken time to investigate the back of the property or the pond.

She went in, loaded breakfast dishes in the dishwasher, wiped down counter tops and the table. She put on her hiking boots and packed a small backpack with a water bottle and snacks, locked the house and headed out the back door.

As soon as she walked out the door, she was glad to have made this choice. The temperature had warmed since the kids had left but it wasn't too warm to go without a jacket. It was going to be a beautiful fall day. The robins and sparrows above her were busy getting ready for the winter. A flock of Canadian geese flew overhead in the shape of a flying V honking their calls back and forth. The breeze whipped at her hair and gave her a little chill. Michigan really is beautiful in the fall. Living in Toledo, Ohio the last few years, she missed the quiet back-roads of her hometown.

The path to the pond was quiet, not an animal to be seen. The only sound was the crackling of branches on the trees as they swayed in the breeze. The colors were even more amazing when she was wrapped in them as she walked under the canopy of leaves. She loved fall. It was a time to think on the past and then let it go. Let the hardships of the year fall to the ground like the leaves, never to return to the tree again. It was time to make room for something new.

Out here in nature she felt closer to God, so this was the time to seek Him out and see what He would show her. So she began to sing praise songs in her mind, then it turned into a hum, then all of a sudden, she was singing at the top of her lungs. Old and new songs. It had been a long time since she felt like singing this way and she was enjoying the presence of the Holy Spirit as she made her way along the path. It was these quiet times that got her through the first five years after Ryan's accident. Without some quiet time with God, she would have fallen apart.

"I wonder how he is doing. God, I hope you have watched out for him like you have for us. I couldn't bear the thought of him living on the streets, or worse. Just be with him. And if you want us back together again, lead him back this way. If not, bring a new man into our lives who will love the kids like his own. More importantly, a man after your heart." She had been praying that prayer every day. Maybe someday she would see the fruit of it.

She finally came to the pond and went out on the fishing dock. She set her bag down and kept singing as she sat there looking around at the tops of the trees and the forest around her. It was amazing out here. She was going to have to make her way out here more.

She started to ponder all God had done for her these past years, even in the lonely times, she knew God was with her. She could feel His presence in those moments of crying herself to sleep. It wrapped around her like a hug. At the same time, she wanted to feel strong arms around her again, arms that did not belong to her sons. Maybe it had been long enough. Maybe she was just afraid to put herself out there again. Stephen was leaving for college in a few years and Aaron was hot on his heels. *Maybe it is time to get serious about dating again?*

Something about that didn't sit right with her. The thought made her feel edgy and uncertain. She couldn't tell if the thought of moving on with another man scared her or if God was telling her "not yet". Something always seemed to stop her. The fact that she never connected with another man the way she had with Ryan spoke volumes to her. Almost a decade was a long time to wait for a stubborn, wounded man. "But he can always change his mind, if he knows I am still waiting for him and love him. Right?"

Suddenly, she had the feeling of someone watching her and then she heard a noise. She looked around her surroundings for something unusual. When her eyes caught sight of movement on the other side of the pond, curiosity kicked in and she got up to walk in that direction. She wanted to know that no one was watching her so she made her way through the fallen trees and branches since there was no path. *You know what they say about curiosity?* "Yes, I know, it killed a cat." Her pulse started to race. Saplings hit her in the legs while she trudged through the brush. At the edge of a clearing, she came to an abrupt halt as she looked in amazement at what was before her. There, in the middle, sat an old barn.

Chapter 7

Decades of misuse shown from roof to the ground. Missing planks, faded paint and a cavernous hole where doors once stood. The old barn leaned to one side and the roof seemed to have caved in showing her the top of a tree protruding out the top of the barn. Once she approached the place where the door once was, she glanced around to see that it was safe and went right in. Sure enough, the roof had caved in, decades ago. There was a tree growing right up the center of the barn. It was beautiful. The sunlight showed in through the rafters and illuminated the tree. "Beautiful!" she said in awe. She wished her camera was working.

She gave her eyes a minute to adjust to the light change and she looked around. There was a sickle hanging on one wall along with horse tack and leather straps. An old yoke hung on another wall. Grass was growing on the dirt floor. There were horseshoes in the corner of one stall. An anvil between another two stalls. In yet another stall, she was shocked at what she found buried. An old buggy. "It's like they left and never came back." She couldn't believe all the treasures that were just on the walls. Makes you wonder what is buried in the dirt. I wonder what happened. I should bring the kids out here and show them this. If I can find my way out of here and then back again. She giggled and then heard footstep. Well, more like a step and a drag. A shiver went up her spine. She turned to look and see if anyone came in behind her.

"Hello! Anyone else here?"

Nothing, and the steps had stopped but she still felt like she was being watched. She hoped it hadn't been an animal. She was in no way ready to leave yet and had no way to defend herself. There was just too much to look at and discover. She went from one stall to the next and was amazed. She thought about going up to the hayloft, but the ladder looked unsafe.

Her stomach made a gurgling sound.

"Guess it is time to eat something." She sat at the base of the tree and pulled out the snack and water from her bag. She couldn't believe how long she had been out here. "I should head back when I am done. This place is so amazing it is hard to pull away." So she just sat there for a while longer.

She closed her eyes and prayed, thought about the kids, thought about her students, what she wanted to change about the house, and then the thinking stopped.

She had fallen asleep. Haunting dreams came flooding in on her; dreams of a garden, a wedding, and Ryan.

He stood at the end of the aisle, waiting for her. He wore a tan suit and she wore a white cotton, eyelet dress. They were surrounded by family and a few close friends. It was a sunny, breezy day. It was warmer than usual for the second day of fall. But Emma was glad for it. It meant no rain on their outdoor wedding.

Fall was a beautiful time of year, especially when standing in Grandmother Daniels' garden. She had the whole yard planted in flowers and trees so that from early spring to late fall, there were blooming flowers. It really did take your breath away. Emma had helped her get the garden ready for this day since the start of summer. They finally finished, the day before, with fresh mums in decorative pots scattered throughout the yard. As Emma stepped out of the house and into the backyard, she had to pause a moment and take in the scene all around her. It truly was a glorious day.

"You okay, Pumpkin?" daddy asked. She was daddy's little girl and she could tell he was worried about her due to her age. Nineteen was young to marry, but she didn't care, she felt ready. She and Ryan were together all through high school and were ready for this next step.

"I am fantastic, Daddy! Let's do this!" she told him.

As she walked toward Ryan and their future together, she saw his lips pucker up a little bit and a slight whistle came out. One of those that indicated he had been holding his breath a bit and had just released the air before he passed out. She responded with a little giggle and a bigger smile.

He looked so handsome that she couldn't believe this was their time. His pale green shirt highlighted his hazel green eyes so nicely. He had combed his beautiful dark locks the way she liked. His hair was just a little on the long side. His smile was that of a young man eager for adventure, with his lovely wife at his side of course. He was much taller than the rest of the men in her family, and was strong and lean. When he held her close, his arms encased her like a cocoon. She loved being in that place. There was safety there. Honestly, he was a giant compared to her five foot two stature, but it never bothered her. He was her gentle giant. And she loved him helplessly and unconditionally.

Her dad handed Ryan her hand, he looked him right in the eyes with an intimidating glare and said loud enough for everyone there to hear, "I like you Ryan, and I am trusting you to take care of my baby girl, but here is your one and only warning. You hurt my baby, I will make you disappear. Understand me, son?" With a wink and a peck on the cheek for her, he went and stood with her mother.

Emma could feel Ryan's hand tremble under hers as they approached Pastor Cross. The three of them stood under the homemade arch that was made of branches and twigs. It was made by their brothers and it took many hours. Pastor Cross smiled at them, saw how nervous Ryan was after her dad's warning, and slapped him hard on the shoulder and said,

"Smile son, today is a good day. BUT, I would listen well to her daddy's warning. I would not put anything past him. You should see what he did to the last guy." There was a rolling laughter that came from their guests, and the pastor began.

It was a quick little ceremony and before they knew it, Pastor Cross said, rather loudly, "I now pronounce you Mr. and Mrs. Ryan David Daniels! What God brings together, let no man tear apart. Ryan, you may now kiss your beautiful bride!" They faced the each other and what she thought was going to be a chaste little kiss, like they had agreed on, turned out to be a deep kiss full of all the love and longing they could possibly possess. Breathing became hard and Emma felt everything around her spin. The kiss received cheers and applause and a few "catcalls" from the guests. Pastor Cross had to remind them that they were not alone and to save some for later. With a giggle of embarrassment mixed with excitement, they parted. Before looking at their friends and family, Emma said to Ryan, "From this moment on, it will always be you for me, no one else!"

A lone tear fell from the corner of Ryan's eye but his face shown with all the joy in his heart, "And always you for me."

As they walked back to the house, they were still gazing into each other's eyes. Longing to be alone yet happy to have family and friends around them, they had not even noticed other people around them. It was just them, promising each other forever.

A snapping twig made her jump and brought Emma out of her dream. Her mind felt hazy as it focused in on where she was.

She sat there under the tree. Alone. No Ryan to have and hold. No daddy for their kids. No always and forever. "You promised me," She whispered into the cold air. She imagined that her words were carried out of the barn with the breeze and that he would hear them, wherever he was. She began to sob like it had happened yesterday. Her chest ached with every breath as the weight of the last eight years sat there, reminding her of all that was lost. The hardships would have been different if he had stayed, but they would have gotten through it together. They had all the support they could ever need in each other and their families. "How could you leave us? Leave me? Your 'Always' turned into 'Alone'."

She got up to stretch and wipe her eyes. She picked up her pack, which felt heavier than before though there was nothing in it. It was like all that has been weighing on her filled that pack. She would have to bear that weight no matter what because there was no one there to carry it for her.

But there is.

"Yes, I know. God can carry it and me through all of this. But right now, I just can't", and she made her way out of the barn. She was mad and confused, and right now, in this moment, she wanted to stay that way for a bit longer. She wanted to rage against someone and he wasn't here for her to beat her fist on and to yell at.

Let it out, you'll feel better. Then you can give it to Me to take care of.

"No. I need to keep my cool, for the kids. For myself." She was afraid of what she would say and do if she let it all out at once. She was afraid that she would go over the edge and into pure madness if she let herself feel all that she held inside.

She knew it wasn't good to hold on to the emotions she had raging through her like a herd of wild horses, but she was worried she would not stop raging if she started. That always led to taking it out on those around her, like the kids. She did that for the first year, and though they are older now, it still wasn't fair to them.

***

He stayed in the shadows while she slept and he had to smile that she still would talk in her sleep. What he heard her say as she walked out of the barn though erased that smile just as quick. She was still mad and felt, what was the word she used? *"Alone"*.

He continued to follow her through the trees until she made it to the house. He was surprised where she was living. *Things must be going well for her.* The Peterson place was worth a quarter million at least.

He was caught off guard by his need to want to protect her. He felt like a peeping tom, but he couldn't pull himself away, especially now that he knew that the two properties met at the old barn.

He had been out for his nightly walk about the property that the house he rented was on. It was part of his therapy so that his muscles didn't tighten too much. Sometimes he would wander to Old Man Peterson's pond to think and he was surprised to see her sitting on the dock. He didn't know the Peterson place was even up for sale. He couldn't turn around when he heard her singing. He had always thought that she sounded like an angel and to hear her voice again was like a healing salve on the wounds of his heart. It felt good, but it hurt too. He wanted to go to her and hold her again, but he wanted her to live her life. Since he couldn't be closer to her, he would hide in the shadows of the trees.

When she got up from the dock and walked around the pond in his direction, he had to really duck and hide. He followed her to the old barn. He watched her as her curiosity took over and as she decided to sit and take a break. He had gotten a kick out of hearing her talk to herself. He was glad some things never changed.

When she fell asleep, he felt brave enough and moved toward her. He wanted to get as close as possible without waking her. He wanted to inhale the scent that she wore so well, citrus and vanilla, and remember. Maybe it would give him the courage he needed to face her but then he heard her mumble and so he jumped back and on the way out the door stepped on a twig. It was close, but worth it.

Now, he stood in her backyard just inside the tree line of her yard. She walked through the house and turned on lights as she went from one room to the next. Finally, she turned on the light to the back bedroom. *Must be hers. God I miss her. Why did you let me do it?*

Pastor Cross had reminded him that "God doesn't make you do one thing or another. He gave us free will." Well he sure practiced that. It was what he thought was best but the more he watched her and listened to her talk to herself in the barn, he realized that was not the case. So what are you going to do now? He wasn't sure, but he felt the urgency to fix what he tore apart eight years ago. "God, show me what to do. I can't live without them anymore. I'll do whatever you want me to do." He would do what he could to make it up to his family.

The next day, David woke with determination and drove to the church. He had to talk to Pastor, and God, too.

As he pulled in the parking lot, he didn't see any cars so he sat and waited for Pastor to get there. He would wait for a few minutes and then go looking for him. While he sat there, he saw a red late model SUV drive by. It reminded him of a time when she said she wanted a bright red SUV or truck. He teased her about it. He told her jokingly, "Why? So the oncoming traffic can see you coming from a mile away.

Then they would have time to get out of your way." She had been so mad at him. He never found out why she wanted one, but he now had a feeling that the big red SUV was her and the kids. It was about the right time to get the kids to school. She must be doing well for herself and the kids.

He thought about following them, but then thought better of it. If it wasn't them he would look like a predator of some kind. He would just stay right here and wait. Besides, if he really thought about it, his scars had actually scared her and the kids. I can't ask them to go through that. I can't ask them to live with the man who looks like some horror flick monster. "What am I doing? I can't tie them down to this monster."

Just as he decided to leave and forget about having a talk with his mentor and friend, the man pulled into the parking lot. David started the truck up again and pulled out of the parking spot. Just as he was passing Pastor Cross, the man waved him down.

"What are you doing here so early, David?"

"Oh I thought I needed to talk to you, but, um, I think I have things figured out."

"Are you sure? You don't sound too sure."

"Yeah, man. I'm good. Have a good one." David got out of there as quickly as he could. He was not going to talk to anyone about his plans from last night. In fact, he was going to forget them altogether. He had decided he was not going to bind her and the kids to his life, they deserved so much better than him. "I need to do everything I can to push them out of my mind. It is better for them this way."

He had made his choice; just like he did eight years ago. This time though, there was no heartache, because they didn't even know where he was. Well, maybe for them at least.

Chapter 8

It was October second and another wedding anniversary without him. Emma had gone through the last couple of years faintly remembering what today was. She wondered if coming back here was bringing it all back to the front of her memory. All those wonderful moments in their lives. She hated days like today were crippling to her. She wanted to forget and move on. But something wouldn't let her.

It has been a long couple of weeks at the school and now that all her students were comfortable with her, they were showing their true colors. She was glad her own kids were starting to settle down again. The fighting was tapering back and the boys were not at constant war with each other like they were. They had their moments, but who was she to complain.

The boys had been doing their fair share of help in the yard and around the house. They had gotten things winterized and had been doing a beautiful job mowing and trimming the yard each week. They had been making sure they kept their things in order and had even started to do their own laundry. She wondered who had given them a talking to, but she had a feeling her dad had given them that "man up" talk that she had heard him give her brother once. Sarah was even starting to help out a bit more around the house, but her little eight-year-old brain could only focus for so long before she was off doing something else.

This last week had her looking for some resemblance of peace and quiet, so she let the kids take a walk through the property and just have some fun. She was determined that today would be a relaxing kind of day. She was standing at the kitchen sink, finding that it was very calming doing dishes by hand. Her dishwasher was making a funny noise and she had called for a repairman last night and was told he would be by today. The dishes were piling up, so she turned up the music that was playing the living room while she went to work.

She was startled when the front screen door slammed shut and she heard a familiar voice shout at her over the music. She turned to greet her dear friend, Ann.

"Hey Lady! I am back here. The radio is by the TV if you want to turn it off so we can chat.

I am up to my elbows in soap suds." She heard the music turn off, "Thanks a bunch."

"May I ask why you are washing your dishes by hand when your dishwasher is right next to you?" Ann asked as she walked into the kitchen with two coffees from the local coffee shop. "Oh, coffee!" Emma replied eagerly while wiping her hands dry. "You must have read my mind." She took a sip and answered the question. "It is making a funny noise and dumped water all over my floor the other day. I have a repair guy coming by sometime today to look at it."

"Who did you call?"

"It's a name Pastor Cross gave me. I had met him once before. David?"

"Good, he does a wonderful job. He didn't give you a time though? That isn't like him."

"No time, but he said it wouldn't be too late in the day."

"So, you have time to catch up?"

"Sure do, let's go out back. The kids went for a walk and I want to keep an eye out for them." They made their way out to the back porch and got comfy in her matching Adirondack chairs. They were almost as comfortable as her porch swing.

"So how are things going? Everyone settling in?" Ann asked to start things off.

"Not too bad. Kids have been great the last couple of weeks. The students, though, have me ready to bolt outta there." Emma replied with a giggle.

"I bet. So how are you doing?" The word *'you'* was stressed like it had an underlying meaning. What she was really asking was "How are you holding up?"

Emma took a deep breath, "Oh, good I suppose. I was in no way ready for the emotions I would come across moving back home. For example, today would have been our fourteenth wedding anniversary. This day has come and gone for the last few years without any thought that was linked with emotion. But this morning, I woke up and started to cry once I realized what day it was. I hate it."

"You think maybe you just repressed so much that now it is overflowing and you have to just let it all out?"

"Ann, don't psycho analyze me right now. I am not in a good place to do it."

"Sometime when you think you are not in a place to do it that is when you need to. Have you prayed about it?"

"Yes I have. I have a pretty good idea why. I know there are things I never dealt with."

"So when are you?" Her friend was grinning at her like she knew she had Emma caught by the nape of the neck. Emma hated being in this place.

Just as she was about to respond, she heard the sound of a vehicle coming down the driveway followed by shouts from one of her kids. She shot up out of her chair and dumped her coffee and ran around to the front of the house.

Turning the corner of the house, she saw a smoky colored Silverado parked in her drive. A large man jumped out of the truck and as quickly as possible, he limped to the back of the truck. Her mind was racing with different scenarios. The worst was at the forefront of her mind. What did he do to my kids?

"What happened? What did you do to my kids?" Emma hollered at the man she recognized to be David.

Sarah came running to her, "No Mama, it isn't him. He helped. We found a doggie!" Her baby girl looked like she had been crying a bit.

Emma looked up at David and realized he had an alert but whimpering mutt of a dog in his arms. He walked up to her, "Is he yours? The kids said he was."

"Oh really?" She stared pointedly at each of her little story tellers. Placing her hands on her hips she asked, "Since when did we get a dog?"

Stephen stepped forward and sheepishly replied, "We found him a week ago in the woods and have been feeding him the leftovers."

"So that's where they went. I thought you were going through another growth spurt." She looked at David. "What happened?"

"I found the kids huddled around him by the road. I stopped to see if I could help and they told me his leg was hurt. Listen I know how to clean and bandage this poor guy up if you don't mind offering your home as a safe place for him. I know whose dog it is and that person is gone. He moved a week ago. He is a pampered pup who found good friends just in time. Besides, he is awfully heavy and I need to put him down."

She stood there for a moment, looking at all four hopeful faces. She had the burly stranger begging for her to be a refuge for someone else's dog and the kids were right there with him. This all felt familiar to her but she wouldn't let herself go there right now.

"Okay! Fine! Aaron, go get bandages. Stephen, get whatever Mr. David tells you he needs. Sarah, you just pet and talk to the poor guy. I'll be right in." She looked up at David and gave him a look that said, "And you better be as good as people say you are."

He looked right back at her, "They will be fine ma'am." And they all walked in to the house. She turned around and walked back to the back porch.

"Well, drama returns to my doorstep. I guess we will have to hold this off." Ann stood to give Emma a hug.

"It's okay girl. It was good while it lasted."

Ann walked to her car and Emma went inside. She did not want to do this today. She wanted relaxation and peace. Unfortunately, it looked like she wasn't going to get it.

***

He didn't look up when Emma walked through the back door, but he knew every move she made behind him. He was distracted by the fact that he could be so in-tune to her movement. He heard her turn on the faucet and fill the kettle. He knew she wouldn't drink coffee in the afternoon, but a day like this called for some hot tea. He was so distracted by her, he lost track of what he was doing for the poor dog he was bandaging.

"Mr. David?" The small, meek voice broke the spell.

"Yeah, sweetie?"

"Will the doggie die?" Her tenderness broke his heart.

"No, I don't think so."

"What do you think happened?" Emma was at his left with Sarah between the two of them.

"Looks like maybe a dog fight. We have a lot of wild dogs in these woods." He looked up at Emma to stress his next words. "It isn't really a safe place for someone to be walking around out there after a certain time of day. They will attack humans as well as other animals. They are a mean bunch." He hoped she got his point. "So this guy's name is Max. His previous owner moved away to the next town over to a nursing home and couldn't take the dog but knew no one to take him. His family didn't want the mutt so they just let him go. It is a shame, because Max is a pretty good dog. Aren't ya, boy?" The last part he said as he gently stroked the dog's head and back. Sarah had been scratching the dogs head and chin, talking to him calmly. It had helped when he had to shave around the dog's wound.

He caught movement out of the corner of his left eye. "Is this my razor?" Emma held it up in a scolding manner, "You had to use my one and only razor?"

"Sorry mom. Mr. David said he needed to shave around the wound and it was the only one I could find." Aaron stated to his mildly perturbed mother.

"I guess" was all she said while she walked to the sink to clean it as best as she could.

"Mom? Can we keep him?" Stephen asked humbly.

She turned and looked at all three of them. "Are you going to take care of him? Bathe him, feed him and walk him? I'll not have him using my house as a bathroom."

In unison, they replied, "YES!" David had to chuckle at the eager faces. She had done well on her own.

With a defeated huff, she replied, "Alright. But here is your warning, okay? You do the work and take care of him. And my bedroom and the back room are off limits, understand?"

"Yes mom!"

"Okay take him outside and find a rope for a lead for now. After David looks at the dishwasher, we will go get supplies."

David lifted the dog off the kitchen island and put him carefully on the floor. "Take care, boy. I think you have a good family now," he said to the dog as he ruffled the fur on the dog's head and it limped out the door with the kids. David and Emma laughed in unison at the happy limping dog and bouncing children.

David turned to Emma and just watched her wipe down the counter and start to take care of things. "Well, I guess you have another job you need tending too?"

"Yup. Right there next to the sink." She continued to tell him what was wrong with the dishwasher but he only half heard her. He knew exactly what was wrong, but he just wanted to stand there and look at her and hear her talk to him. He was amazed that the scars had not changed the way she treated him. She didn't shy away or anything. It felt nice to not have to lower his head or turn his face in another direction for fear of frightening someone.

He was still looking at her when he noticed her lips stopped moving. She was giving him a curious look now. Guess it was time to work. "I have a pretty good idea what it is and it won't take much to fix it. I'll get it taken care of and be out of your way within an hour or so."

"Great! Sounds good. I'll just be in my office grading papers."

"I'll find you if I need you" he told her. But as he said "I need you" something like a switch flipped in his heart, telling him he needed her alright, but not to inspect his work on the kitchen appliance. He needed her in his life again. *Maybe I should at least tell her. She deserves to know. So do the kids. I won't be asking to be a constant fixture in their lives, but they need to know who I am. That I am alive.* He knew that it couldn't happen the way he really wanted things to be. *I can dream though, can't I?* This would be the longest hour ever.

Chapter 9

A week later, David found himself pulling into Emma's driveway yet again. He didn't know what possessed him to come here, but here he was. He had a Barbie toy wrapped in pretty pink paper sitting on the seat next to him.

Last week, while taking the kids and the injured dog, Max, back to the house, Sarah had sat in the front seat with him and chatted away. It was a moment that he felt blessed to have. He knew it would be a rare moment in his life with his daughter, even if she didn't know who he was to her.

During her ramblings and chatter, she had mentioned that her birthday was back in August, but because of the move they couldn't celebrate it. So today she was having a party with all her new friends. As he stepped out of his truck, he could hear the squeal of little girls coming from the backyard. It warmed his heart to know that his daughter had found some friends.

He walked up the front steps to the door and gave a knock. While he was waiting for someone to answer the door, he turned to look out over the field across the road. Emma truly had a beautiful view from here. From where he stood-facing the house, the swing was to the right of the front door with a wicker side table. On top rested a potted plant. Her coffee cup next to the plant. He could imagine her sitting on her front porch with her coffee in her hand and a look of peace on her face, maybe even a slight smile as well.

He heard in a hushed male voice say "Ryan?" Dread hit him in the chest. He looked back to the door to find Emma's dad standing on the other side. His heart began to race in fear of being found out.

How does he know? Now what?

"My name is David, sir." Maybe he could fool him. The look in the old man's eyes told him he hadn't. David was amazed at how aged his former father-in-law was. He was a good man. Realizing how old he was getting added a bit of sadness to his terror. *If he figured it out, has Emma?*

The man charged the door with so much force that it made David back up and almost fall off the porch steps. The man grabbed him by the arm and dragged him off to one side of the porch where no one could see or hear them.

David was shocked by the old man's strength. Old but not fragile.

"Don't try and fool me boy! I know exactly who you are, even if you tell everyone else you are David. What are you doing here? Do Emma and the kids know you are here?"

He never could fool this man. He was too smart for David's own good. Trying to waste more time so he could figure out what to say, he stepped a little further away from the door. He turned to the patriarch and hung his head in shame. There would be no hiding from this man.

"Sir, um, no Emma doesn't know it's me. She sees the scars and hears David. She never saw me in the hospital without the bandages. And I want to keep it that way." David was truly worried that his former father-in-law was going to say something now. He couldn't let that happen. "Tom, sir, you can't tell her. I'm a crippled monster of a man who sees she is doing well for herself. I don't want to burden them with this, so I wish to remain 'David' to them. At least for now. Please promise me you will not say anything."

He could see the gears turning behind the man's eyes. He never knew him to be dishonest, but he also knew that the man was wise. He hoped he knew that this way was the best for the people they both loved.

"Ryan, you and I both know she needs to know. The kids need to know. Son, they won't turn you away." Tom had moved closer to David and put a firm hand on his shoulder and lightly squeezed. It was actually very comforting to David in a way.

"I'll think about it, but I am not ready for them to know. And, I am not trying to sound like a know-it-all, but it is not your place to tell. Let me do it in my time."

With a heavy sigh, the man agreed. "So how did you know where they lived? And judging from the pink package in your hands, you know this is Sarah's party. How did you find out about it?"

"I was here just last week to fix her dishwasher. I am known around here as a handyman. On my way here, I came across the kids hovered around a wounded dog and in transporting them and the dog here, Sarah mentioned that her party was this weekend. I saw this doll in the store and it made me think of her, so here it is." He reluctantly handed it to the man the package, deciding it would be best to just go. He wanted to see his girl's face when she opened it, but knowing she had it would be enough. "Can you make sure she gets this? I should get going?"

"Ryan, stay and give it to her yourself." He tried to hand it back to him but he wouldn't take it back. David put his hands up and stepped away.

"No, it would just be better this way. Honestly, I am not quite sure what I was thinking coming here for anything other than a repair job. I gave up my rights eight years ago."

"Yes, you did, but there are always second chances. I can see God has given you a second chance. What makes you think they won't?"

Okay, this was getting too deep. "I don't expect them to." He started down the steps, and then he heard Emma call him as she came through the door.

"David! Hi! What brings you here?" *Shoot!*

"Oh, well, um, Sarah told me last week that she was having a birthday party today, so I brought her a little something. Your dad was going to give it to her for me."

"Well, why don't you come in and give it to her yourself? Have some cake and ice cream."

"No, I would like to, but I can't. Have a good time."

With a wave and the desire to run, he quickly made his way to his truck, got in and made his way out of the driveway. Once he hit the road, he let out the breath he didn't realize he was holding. He never expected people to recognize him. He was surprised Emma hadn't. She knew him better than anyone. *Maybe she just chooses not to see it.*

He knew he had hurt her. Every time he saw her, he could see the hurt in her eyes. He hated seeing her like that. He had hoped she had moved on and found someone new, but clearly not. He didn't want to hold out hope that she was waiting for him but there was a part of him that hoped that was the case. Only time would tell. There had to be a reason God had orchestrated things the way they were going.

***

She was shocked to see David standing on her front porch talking to her dad. As soon as she stepped out on to the porch, she could feel the tension between them. They had been deep in conversation and whatever her dad said to him had David bolting for his truck. He couldn't seem to get out of here fast enough.

"Dad, what did you say to him?"

Her dad was never a shifty or uncertain man. He knew his mind and he knew how to say things. You never wondered what he was thinking. But right now, he seemed very hesitant to answer her question.

"Dad, do you know David?"

"Kind of. He grew up around here. I used to see him a lot, but this is the first time in a long time," her dad finally told her.

"Who is he? He told me he grew up here but I can't figure out who he is. The name isn't familiar."

"Well, Pumpkin, it is his story to tell," as he patted her arm. "Let's go have some cake."

He walked into the house and just left her hanging. She could tell he knew something, but he obviously was not going to tell her so she decided to not push it and get back to the party.

Chapter 10

Halloween. Emma hated the so called holiday. She hated the masks in the stores and the yard decorations that she saw as she drove to and from school. She hated the feeling of fear that just hung in the air, or maybe it was just her own fears creeping up on her. The kids, well they loved dressing up and going door to door asking for candy. Thankfully, her brother and sister-in-law had saved her from having to go into town. *Ah, yes, here they are*, she thought as she watched them pull in.

"KIDS! Uncle Dan and Aunt Heidi are here! Let's go!"

"Mom! I can't find my wig!" Sarah was dressed as a princess and needed her long blond wig.

"I saw it last on the couch," she heard Aaron holler down the hall.

"Got it!" Sarah replied.

The sound of a herd of thundering elephants roared over her head and then down the stairs. The kids reached the door and she was kissed on the cheek by each of them. They grabbed the trick -or- treat bags she handed them and ran for the vehicle.

Heidi walked up the porch steps, well at least tried to as Stephen, Aaron, and Sarah tried to go down the steps. The sight made Emma giggle. Things are back to normal. Maybe even better than normal. She was uneasy moving back to her hometown, but now she was realizing it was a long overdue thing. The kids loved being here.

"Hey girl! Anna and Jake want your three to stay the night tonight. You okay with that?"

"Oh, well you want me to bring bags for them?"

"We have extra toothbrushes and it isn't like the kids are so different in sizes that they can't wear each other's clothes."

"Well, if you don't mind, then I guess. Make sure they brush their teeth before bed. And please, only one piece of candy tonight. Sarah will be impossible to get to sleep."

"Not a problem." Heidi gave Emma a hug. "They will be just fine. Have a good night and enjoy the quiet." Heidi gave her an awkward wink, like she knew something, and moved down the steps.

Emma waved and blew a kiss to them as they drove away. She loved the quiet, but she started second guessing herself and how she acted around her family they were always taking the kids for her. Was she acting overwhelmed or stressed?

She walked around the house to inspect the gardens. She had a few fall plants still thriving and blooming and she enjoyed her flowers. It was a little hobby she and Ryan had together and she just never stopped. There were always plants somewhere around the house.

The phone rang inside. So she ran in and tripped a bit on the steps, "OUCH!" She hobbled into the house just as the phone stopped ringing. She reached for it and looked at the caller ID: *Ann Adams*. She pushed dial and called her back.

"Hey girl! What's up?" Emma asked as she rubbed her throbbing shin.

"Well, some of us ladies are going to karaoke night at the Rocking Horse. It has been a long time since we all have gotten together and a little bird told me that you would have no kids at all tonight and, well, I know how you hate to be alone. So what do you say?" *So that's what the wink was for!*

"Oh, Ann, I don't know. It has been a long time. I thought about just hiding out here and enjoying the quiet. Maybe get some reading done." She heard laughter on the other end.

"Honey, that is the point of me calling. You lock yourself in that big house with you and your little chicks and you do very little socializing. So come on. I'll even drive."

Emma let out a heavy sigh as she contemplated the proposal. It did sound like a lot of fun. It had been a long, long time since she had a night out, let alone a girl's night.

"Emma? You still there?"

"Yeah, I am here. I guess I am in."

"Woo-hoo! She is in, ladies!" Emma heard Ann yell to whoever was with her. "Oh by the way, you have to wear a costume to get in free of charge."

"A costume? How old are we? How about I wrap myself in toilet paper and I can be a mummy." That was lame Em! She chastised herself.

"Oh you need this outing more than we thought. Think young for a bit, you are not a mom tonight, but just Emma. Come up with something and we will be there in an hour."

"Okay. See you soon. I make no promises." And they hung up the phone. *A costume. Good grief.* With a heavy sigh, she walked up the stairs.

She did not want to dress up, but she would give it her best shot. As she stood in front of her closet, she stared into the cavern of clothing. She wasn't sure if she even had anything she could fake it with. Looking up to the top of the closet, she saw a box that said "Ryan" on it. It was full of a few of Ryan's things that she was not willing to give up. She lowered the box, pulled off the tape and opened it up. First thing she saw was his favorite ball cap with his favorite college football team logo on it. She traced the "M" with her finger. A knot formed in her belly and moved up her throat. *Don't go there right now Emma. You don't have time.* She pushed the feeling to sob back down and put the hat on her head. She dug a little further and found the matching sweatshirt. *Yeah, I'll go as a football fan.* She kicked the box back into the closet and changed shirts. She went into the bathroom, and using Sarah's hair ties, put her hair in pigtails. *Yup, this will have to work.* As long as she didn't think about what she was wearing and whose it really was, she would have a good night.

She needed something more.

"Face paint!" She went to the hall closet and got Sarah's face paint out and painted an "M" on her cheek in blue and yellow. It was hard since it was in the mirror, but it would have to do. She put the ball cap back on and looked long and hard at herself in the mirror. She needed this night, no matter how much she didn't want to go.

If she was honest with herself, she would admit that she was ready for something different. *Maybe no frumpyr Emma? Maybe I will meet someone. Lord that would be nice. Someone who would take care of me like I take care of everyone else.* She was tired of kid conversations all the time. She was tired of being the only adult in the house. She was tired of doing this parenting thing on her own.

The doorbell rang and Ann shouted through the door for Emma to hurry up. "Well, no backing out now," she said to herself as she grabbed money off the dresser and put her license in her back jean's pocket and pranced down the stairs to the door. Though she had no plans to drink, they still carded you.

"You ready?" Ann asked with excitement in her voice.

"You bet. It is time for a 'Mom's Night Out'." She put her hand on Ann's arm to stop her for a second as they stepped off the last step, "Don't let me be a silent wallflower. I need this no matter how reluctant I am."

"Glad you have recognized that. Now let's go!"

They climbed in the van and she saw a full vehicle of all her old friends, including Tiffany, Ryan's younger sister. "What are you doing here?" Emma asked with excitement. She hadn't seen any of his family since she moved here.

"Ann called me and told me what she had in mind. I was not going to pass this up. Brad practically pushed me out the door. Sorry I haven't come to see you yet. Forgive me?"

"If you do a duet with me tonight," she said with a teasing tone and an arched brow.

"You got it."

"Okay! Buckle up Diva Emma so we can go!" she heard from the back.

"Is that you Erica?" Emma could barely see clear to the back.

"Yes Ma'am! Now let's go, I want to do some singin' and dancin'!"

This was going to be a good night.

***

Another group of ladies walked in. The bar was really busy tonight with all the singles or those who had no kids waiting for them at home. David hated working the bar on nights like this, but his boss needed an extra hand. David worked four different jobs around town, plus he had become the "Go To" man for home repairs and quick car repairs for those who had no one to do it for them. The bar job was one he hated to do the most, this wasn't his life anymore, and his sponsor told him it wasn't a good idea but it helped pay the bills.

With a heavy sigh, he turned to hand a guy his drink and was staring her in the face. He hadn't seen Emma walk in. He handed the guy the glass, cleared his throat of the frog that took residence there every time he *saw her, and asked, "What can I get for ya?"* WOW! *She looks beautiful when she dresses down. Wait, is that my hat and hoodie?*

He couldn't believe she had kept them.

"Um, just a soda."

"Hey! What is taking so long? Come on Em, we have to pick our song." When David looked up from pouring the drink, and saw his sister at the bar next to Emma. He put the glass down for Emma as quick as he could and then turned and walked to the other end of the bar. He was still reeling from Emma's dad figuring out who he was, he knew his sister would too.

"I have an order to place, Bud!" Tiffany yelled at him down the bar. *She always did have a big mouth.* He signaled to another bartender to wait on her. It was going to be hard to avoid the whole party, but he would do what he could.

He had a hard time not watching Emma the whole night. The fact that she was here for karaoke was a bonus. He loved to hear her sing. It was hard not to stop and stare when she walked up to the microphone. She smiled at the DJ to indicate she was ready and David had to remind himself to breathe. That smile still took his breath away.

It was a joy to see her have a good time. The fact that a bunch of church ladies descended on the bar was a shock for him, but it was a breath of fresh air. They were all loud and crazy and not intoxicated. They were all just as fun to watch, but Emma stole the show for him.

His bar partner must have caught him watching Emma, because he walked over and made an off color remark to him about her. David turned to the guy with a smile plastered on his face to make the guy think he agreed, but then made the smile disappear and replied, "You touch her, I'll make you hurt, for life. I may have Jesus in my life, but I'll not let you lay a hand on her."

"Wow! Someone is touchy. Do you know her? Or do you have plans to go after her yourself?"

"I do know her, from church. I respect her, and all those ladies she came in with. When you wait on them, you better pretend you're a choirboy and behave yourself. Got it?"

He made sure he gave the guy a pointed look to make it clear that he would hold the guy to it. He gave a nod, made another unrepeatable remark and walked away. David didn't care what the guy thought of him. He wasn't here to play nice, but do a job.

Halfway through her song, Ann jumped up and almost ran to Emma and handed her a cell phone. The hairs on the back of his neck stood up. He could sense something was wrong. Emma looked down at where Ann pointed and then she dropped the microphone while trying to put it in the stand and ran out the door. The room was filled with a loud squeal as the microphone was dropped and people cringed.

He went for his jacket in the back room and ran out the front door. That's when he ran right into Tiffany.

"Umpf!"

"Sorry"

"It's okay, Ryan. You had better follow me."

He froze just outside the door and stared at his sister as she jogged down the sidewalk.

"Wait? What?" He asked. He knew she would eventually figure it out as well, but he didn't think she had noticed in such a dark room.

"You! Follow! NOW! It's Sarah!"

That put power in his feet and he ran to the truck best as he could. By the time he climbed inside the truck, his leg was starting to throb. He turned the keys he had put into the ignition, slammed the truck into gear and squealed his tires as he sped out of the parking spot. His mind raced almost as fast as he drove the truck. Something was wrong with his baby girl.

He stayed a block behind all the way to the hospital. Until he knew how bad it was, he would stay in the shadows. When he got to the hospital, he saw his sister at the front entrance and she stopped him.

"Hold on brother dear." He knew the tone, she was mad, most likely at him.

"I need to know what happened to Sarah, Tiff!" He was about to blow and he didn't care at this point who knew who he was. His baby needed him.

"Before I tell you a thing, you have to answer a question."

"I don't want to play games. By the way, how did you know it was me?"

"I lived across the hall from you for 15 years and then I babysat the boys until Emma moved out of town. I can spot you a block away. I have known you were around town for the last six months. I've just been waiting for you to come out of the woodwork. Now my turn. WHERE IN THE WORLD HAVE YOU BEEN!?" She punched him in his left shoulder. It startled him but he figured he deserved it.

"In hiding! Look at me, Tiff! Now, what happened to Sarah!?" His blood was boiling right now and he was about to take it out on someone if he didn't get answers, soon.

"We will talk more later." She let out a sigh, he guessed, to clear her head. "She had a fall at Emma's brother's. He and his wife were nice enough to keep the kids for the night so we could get Emma out of the house. Well, Sarah apparently had a fall down the stairs while sleepwalking. That is all I know right now. I have no clue how bad the break is yet. Now are you going to come in or are you going to stay out here?"

He thought about it for a second. He could feel the fear coming on. It started in his stomach like a rock weighed it down, and then it started to creep up into his throat. *God, I can't. Not yet. I just can't.* "Will you come out here and report to me when you know? I can't yet"

With an irritated sign, his sister nodded her head and walked to the door. She turned before she walked through the doors, looked straight at him and said, "You're a fool, you know that right? Your daughter would love nothing more than to have her daddy hold her in this kind of situation and you are too caught up in your fear to come into the light. I love you big Bro, but you are a fool." With that said, she turned back to the door and went into the hospital.

He sat on a stone bench by the door. He figured his heart weighed about as much as the bench. He knew his sister was right. He was a fool and a coward. He put his head in his hands and began to pray for his baby girl and his family.

He sat on that bench for a few more minutes and then he decided to leave. He couldn't do anything here. Plus, he had to answer to his boss. That was going to be fun to explain.

***

Emma felt like she was going to fall apart at any moment. Her baby was hurt and she couldn't do a thing about it. All she could do was sit and hold Sarah's left hand while they wrapped her right. She would have to have someone write for her at school for the next few weeks. She heard a little whimper come out of her baby girl and she wanted to whimper right along with her. Emma felt bad, but she was just a little bit envious of her daughter because Emma had no one to turn and cry into. She had managed to go eight years without a major accident and all this one did was bring back all the memories of Ryan's.

Emma was watching the nurse wrap Sarah's arm when a hand touched her shoulder. She was so focused that she jumped a little and looked at a man who had hair the color of wheat. I t was just a little long but looked well maintained and his eyes were the color of the ocean. His skin was tanned just enough that he had a bronze glow about him. He smiled at her and his teeth were so white... oh, who was she kidding, this man was gorgeous! Gorgeous like that movie star she liked to watch. He was one of the stars in those car movies where it was okay to break the law because it served a good purpose. WOW! Was the only thought she could form. If she was dreaming, let her stay that way for just a bit longer.

"Ms. Daniels?"

"Uhh!" She blinked a couple time to wake herself up. "Yes! Just call me Emma."

"Okay, Emma, I am Dr. Emerson. I am the doctor caring for your daughter. I thought I would go over a few things with you since I couldn't touch base with you when you first came in. Can we talk out here in the hall?"

"Oh, yes. Sarah, honey? I'll be right back. I will be right outside."

"Okay, mama." responded Sarah like there was not a care in the world. She was totally calm now. Probably the medication.

"Here I am falling apart and she is acting like it is no big deal. Kids bounce back so quickly," she said to the doctor as they stepped into the hall.

"They do have a wonderful way of doing that. Now, here is the list of medications I am prescribing for her for pain and infection prevention. This sheet is just some things to go over with her on 'do's and 'don'ts' like 'don't put weight on that arm' those kind of things. I noticed you don't have a primary care physician, so if it is okay, I would like to see her on Tuesday or Wednesday. Just to check on her arm and see how she is doing." He must of have noticed her panic because he then said, "and see how you are doing. Here is my card, so you can call me anytime, day or night." He looked down at their feet like a nervous school boy and a bit of red shading was showing over the edge of his collar. It took her a second to figure out his meaning. *Is he hitting on me? Should I be mad or happy that I've still got it. Wait a second...*

"You are making quite an assumption if I get your meaning. How do you know that I don't have a husband at home? I didn't indicate I was single."

"Yeah," he rubbed the back of his neck. She got a kick out of watching this handsome doctor squirm just a bit. "I overheard one of your friends tell the nurse there was no husband or boyfriend when she was asked if we should call anyone else besides you. Sorry if I am out of line."

Well that was sweet and bold. I could admire that. "Okay I will choose not to be offended." She couldn't help but smile at him as he was so humble about it. "Thank you for all your help Dr. Emerson. It means a lot." She gave him her best smile and turned to go back in the room. Dr. Emerson had a few words with Sarah and then released her.

"It was good to meet you Sarah, and your mom." He looked straight at Emma, smiled, and then nodded his head, "Yes! It was very good to meet you." He turned to look back at Sarah, "Now I will be seeing you sometime next week, and take it easy. No climbing trees or hitting any siblings, if you have any."

"I have two older brothers. They're dumb." Sarah rolled her eyes and shook her head while Emma and Dr. Emerson laughed.

"Thank you, Dr. Emerson." Emma held out her hand to shake his. He took her hand, shook it slowly, smiled at her, and then said, "Call me Mike. Less of a mouthful." He winked at Sarah and left the room.

Emma watched him leave as Sarah asked, "Mommy, why did he smile at you like that?"

"Oh honey girl, I don't know. Let's get going." She was not about to talk about this with her eight-year-old daughter. Not tonight. It was late and she was tired.

Chapter 11

Emma called in to the doctor's office first thing Monday morning and the receptionist told her they had an opening for that day. Emma took the appointment and they went in and saw the handsome doctor. She had taken a few days off from work to care for Sarah, so it was no problem, but she did take a couple extra minutes to get ready. Sarah even commented on how her mommy was getting a little too dressy for the doctor's office. She couldn't help feeling like a school girl when it came to Dr. Mike Emerson. A feeling she had not had since high school. It wasn't as strong as it was with Ryan, but it was enough for her to pay attention. It was scary and exciting all at the same time. Maybe it was an indication that she was actually ready to move on. It sure had been long enough.

In the exam room, she and Sarah chatted about school and homework when the handsome doctor walked in. Emma watched him as he took a better look at Sarah's arm and she listened as he asked Sarah questions. She was amazed at how well he connected with her daughter. He had a calming way about him that made it easy for Sarah to talk to him. Usually she had to encourage her daughter to talk to someone.

When he was done wrapping the hard cast, he said to her daughter, "Okay Sarah, why don't you go on out to the nurse's desk and tell Janette I said you can have an extra cookie while I talk to your mommy."

"Okay! I like cookies!" With that she was out the door as fast as she could go.

"She is a beautiful girl, Emma. She looks just like you." There was a bit of a pause before he went into doctor mode. "Okay, I want to see her again in ten days, to check her arm and see how she is doing. I want to make sure she is healthy in her mind as much as in her body."

"What are you looking for when it comes to her mind?" She was unsure of what he meant.

"I want to make sure there is no fear. I want her to feel free to be a kid and not have a fear of falling and hurting herself again." She could understand that. *Smart, caring, and handsome! I hope I am not overreacting but I could use some of that in my life.*

"Emma, I have to ask. Where is Sarah's father? I noticed he isn't listed on the form. If you don't want to tell me, that's okay. Just know that this is Dr. Emerson asking, well and maybe a bit of Mike the guy too, but mostly the doctor." He gave her a shy grin and looked down at Sarah's file. She wasn't sure how to answer this.

"For now, can I just say, he is not in the picture, in any way. I don't think he wanted to leave but I think he felt like he had to leave." She paused, contemplating if she should say more or not, gave a heavy sign, "Yeah, we will just leave it at that for now. It is just a long story."

"Well, Mike," he snickered at himself as he looked at the chart, clearly he felt silly talking about himself in the third person, "would like to know your story better. Dr. Emerson will leave it be for now."

"OH! Well, okay. Mike can call me and, um, we will set something up." This may be the oddest conversation she had ever had with a doctor.

"Great, I will, uh, let him know." They stood and looked at each other, like they were evaluating the seriousness of the other person. Then one of them snorted and then they broke out into a full laugh. As they walked out of the room, everyone stopped to look at was all the commotion was. Once the doctor and Emma noticed that they were being watched, they composed themselves and went back to business. She set the next appointment and with a 'thank you' to all Dr. Emerson's staff, Emma and Sarah left.

In the car, Sarah commented on how silly she was behaving with the doctor. Emma felt the same way. But she realized that Dr. Mike made her feel that way. Like it was okay to be an adult and be a little silly.

When she pulled into the driveway, she noticed David's truck parked by the house.

"Mom! Is that Mr. David's truck?"

"It looks that way."

They got out of the SUV and he got out of his truck with a thermal bag that looked like it was full of some heavy things.

"Hey there. What are you doing here?" Emma asked in a carefree way.

"Um, an act of generosity, perhaps." He hesitated reaching out to shake her hand, but he finally got his hand out there. She reached for his hand to finish the gesture and when their hands connected, a surge of electricity shot up her arm and traveled to her heart. She found herself having a hard time breathing. She quickly looked at him and by the look in his eye, he had the same sensation. They stood there and gazed at each other in amazement.

Sarah's voice broke the gaze. "Ma? Are you okay?"

"Uh. Um. Yeah honey. I … I'm fine." She turned to David, "Why don't you come on in?"

"Please come in and say hi, Mr. David. What ya got in the bag?"

"Well... the pastor asked me to bring this meal by for you. Someone in the church made it and dropped it off. It is really heavy. So yeah, I'll take it in for you." She was shocked at how, considering his appearance, she had no problem trusting this man. After that first meeting, she hadn't felt uneasy around him.

"Yes, please. Come on in and I will show where to put it. Sarah, go on in a head of us and let your brothers know that we have company and to get washed up for dinner." She turned and looked at David. He wasn't looking at her at the moment but was watching Sarah walk in the house. *Hmm. He looks so lost and alone. Why did I not see this before?*

***

He didn't know what possessed him to make the meal and bring it over, but he knew he had to check up on Sarah, the boys and Emma. Ever since Friday at the bar, watching her sing and have fun, and then the need he felt to protect his family, well it just drew him back in to them. He knew he was missing out on a lot, but he didn't realize it until he couldn't be of help to his daughter and Emma.

"If you just put it there on the kitchen island, I'll get plates." He glanced at her and noticed she was watching him, closely. She was studying him; he could feel it. "So, you have been here a couple of times and I have not asked you where you are from, David?"

"Around."

"Where around?" *She won't let it go, guess I better play along.*

"I grew up around here. Was gone for a few years but came back a few months ago. How about you?"

"Hmm, I grew up here too, but I don't recall knowing a David. What year did you graduate?"

He paused for a second. She was getting to close but he was not about to lie. "1998. I was a bit of a loner."

"Okay, well you might have known my husband. Well, ex-husband. He graduated the same year."

"What's his name?"

"Ryan Daniels." His back had been to her because she was setting the table, but he heard her sigh before she said his name. The air had started to feel heavy with tension. He thought maybe he should go but it felt so nice to be in a house with people, especially them.

"Well, I will get going. Let you folks eat. Enjoy the meal."

He walked for the door when he heard a thundering of feet make their way for the dinner table. Stephen stopped in front of him. The look he gave him was the same one Emma had just given him. The kid stuck his hand out at him, "Hi Mr. David! You going to stay for dinner?"

"Well, no, I was just about to leave." The fact that his oldest boy was almost as tall as him shocked him. "Wow! You're a tall one. How old are you?"

"I'm twelve now. Just had a birthday a few months ago."

"Practically a man. What grade are you in this year?"

"Seventh. So, will you stay for dinner?" He had not anticipated this. He had planned to drop things off and go. If he stayed, one of them was bound to figure out who he was. Judging from the look on Stephan's face, someone already had. There was a part of him that wanted them to know and there was a part that said they were better off without him. If this boy was any other boy it would have been easy to walk away. But this wasn't any other boy, it was his boy. His oldest boy. How was he going to turn down his own kid. Do like every other dad does... "What does your mom say? Did you ask her? She may not want company tonight."

Then he heard her from around the corner. "Stephen, you and Mr. David come sit down. You are welcome to stay." She then came around the corner and looked right at him, but not just at him, through him straight to his heart. It was a soft, understanding look like she knew the inner struggle that was raging inside him. "If you would like to stay" she then said. He relaxed just a bit. She was leaving the choice to him.

"Okay, I'll stay. Thank you, Ma'am."

***

She didn't really want him to stay but to not offer after he drove way out here to make a delivery would just be rude. Something about him made her very nervous but not in a negative way. She didn't know what to make of it. He seemed familiar to her, but she couldn't place how. Maybe tonight, she could get closer to figuring it out. If she was truly honest with herself and admit it, she knew exactly who he made her think of - Ryan. She couldn't trust her heart to go in that direction though. She finally felt like she was moving forward.

They all sat down and Stephen said the prayer. As soon as "Amen" was said by all, the room burst with energy as everyone tried to tell her about their day, all at once. Poor David looked overwhelmed as he sat there at the other end of the table. She couldn't help smiling as she watched him. He had a look of pure terror on his face and she thought he was about to jump up and run for the door. "Okay GUYS!!!! Let's take it down a notch. You're scaring Mr. David. He is a guest, let's use our manners."

Each kid, individually, proceeded to tell her about their day, Sarah with great detail. Still though, David looked unsettled and stressed. She needed to practice her manners as well. Make him feel welcome in her home. "Mr. David?" He looked up at her and the sadness in his eyes made her think of Ryan even more. She had to remind her heart that this was not Ryan but a new acquaintance who could be a friend if she would stop her heart from going in another direction. Look past the way he moved and talked and just saw him for who he was. "So, what is it you do for a living?" That was a safe start.

"I guess you can say I am a 'Jack of all trades, but master of none'. I work as a bartender as you know. It isn't my most favorite place to be, but Gary was a friend to me when I first moved here. He was having trouble with keeping order and keeping bartenders out of his till. So he offered me the job until he can find a replacement."

"How long have you worked there?" she asked.

"Six months now." He had a slight grin on his face and a hint of sarcasm in his tone. "I guess he quit looking. That isn't the only thing I do. I do handyman jobs, as you already know, mostly for the little old ladies or single mothers. Um...a little car repair, depending on the age of the vehicle. You will see me around the church from time to time doing odds and ends jobs I manage to make ends meet."

"Wow, you're busy. Don't you have a family to go home to?" Sarah was so sweet.

"No, not right now. I used to." Emma was sure she had seen him shift a bit. He was clearly not wanting to answer that question. After a long pause he continued, "I did have a family but I know they are better off without me, wherever they are."

***

The look Sarah was giving him now was more than he could handle. She had such confusion in her eyes. He could see the storm of questions brewing behind them. Oh to be a child again where everything was so simple.

"How can you say that, Mr. David?" He looked over to Emma, begging her with his eyes, he hoped, to stop the questioning by Sarah.

"Honey, let's leave it be, okay? Mr. David is a guest here. And this is not a time to drill him about his family. Now eat your dinner." She looked at him and gave him a smile that showed her apologies. "I am sorry about my daughter. My husband left us a long time ago, when she was a newborn, and she feels a bit, um ... passionate about being fatherless right now. I am sorry your family is not with you."

"No harm done, nothing I haven't asked myself before." *It's is time to leave. This is too much.* He checked his watch as discreetly as he could.

"Mr. David, I'm sorry." He looked at Sarah in surprise. She sat next to him at the table. Her head was down and she was twisting her fingers. He heard her sniffle and he saw a single tear drop onto her lap. His heart ached to hold her like only a daddy could, but he gave up that right. He felt useless right now.

"I know you didn't mean to hurt me, I can handle it." He looked at Emma looking for a signal of some kind that she trusted him, and put his hand on Sarah's shoulder and patted it, hoping it was somewhat comforting. Like any stranger would do when they saw a young girl crying.

With a little voice, that maybe only he could hear, "Yes, I did. I'm sorry." She looked up at him and then to her mom, "Can I be excused? I feel tired and I have homework." Emma nodded her okay and Sarah stood, turned to him, looked him in the eyes, and then shocked him with a kiss on the cheek, on his scar actually, and hugged his neck. "Good night Mr. David." He managed the proper response through the knot in his throat as he watched her say her good-nights to the rest and leave the room. He really felt like he was intruding now and knew he needed to leave but he just couldn't. Sarah, his daughter, just stole his heart. Again.

"Boys why don't you clean up tonight?" Emma said. He could tell that was not a request. And by the looks of things, so could the boys.

"BUT MOM!"

"No buts, hop to it." Like a drill sergeant, he thought. He had to grin.

It was nice to see her get all feisty again. Too nice. When they were married, he got enjoyment out of riling her up. He would pick on her just to see it. Do whatever he could to make her laugh, most of the time at his own expense. Her laughter was like a drug to him. He needed to hear it every day. If he could get her laughing, he knew all was well. The memory of those times is what kept him going through all the therapy and surgeries on his leg. Those memories kept him fighting. How could he even think he could live this life without her in it? Maybe Emma and David could be friends. Ryan will just have to stay tucked away. He knew just as soon as the thought crossed that it would be difficult, but he would try. *God, I think I am going to need your help with this one.*

Movement beside him caught his attention. It was Emma. She was standing close next to him, too close. She reached for his plate. He felt his pulse start to race. Easy boy, she is just clearing the table. Breathe man! He was really going to have a hard time with this friend thing. It would take as much willpower as he could come up with to resist the urge he had right now to kiss her. Kiss her like he used to every time she came close to him while she would clear the table. He would wrap his arm around her hip and pull her into his lap and then kiss her soundly. The kids were so little at the time that they didn't even notice, but if they had still been married, he gave a slight giggle, they would respond with all the "gross" comments he was now thinking. It would be fun to hear them.

"What's so funny?" He looked up at her. She was smiling at him and it made her eyes glow. His heart began to race in his chest and he found himself mute. She was still a stunning beauty.

"Oh just a thought I had. Here, let me help you." He had to get up and move. It would keep him from doing something he shouldn't.

"No, you don't need to do that. You are a guest. Guests don't clean up after themselves in this house, at least not on the first visit."

He refused to give her his plate, fork and glass. So he stood, grabbed his things and headed for the sink.

"Excuse me sir, did you hear me?" He did, but he was enjoying the rise he was getting out of her. He could hear the humor in her voice as he walked away. He knew she was right behind him because he could feel her staring daggers at him. She was close enough to be in his personal space. He reached the sink and put his dinner dishes in; she was still close to him. Right behind him, it sure wouldn't take much to turn around and... *that's enough. Behave!* The mental reprimand put a smile back on his face. He was enjoying this and he wasn't ready for this night to end. *Funny how one minute I am ready to bolt out of here and the next, I can't bring myself to leave.* Right then an idea formed, "For starters, this isn't my first time here. So, why don't I do the dishes? Let the boys do their homework as I am sure they have some. You can dry." She had a hesitant look on her sweet face. "Let me repay your kindness for letting me stay and have dinner with you all." She gave a heavy sigh and he could see the doubt turning in her brain. He thought she was beautiful when she was like this. He thought she was beautiful all the time.

"Okay. You can wash I'll dry. Soap is under the sink. Let me go get the kids settled and check on Sarah." She turned away to head for the stairs then turned back to him, "Thank you" she said. "Not a problem."

Chapter 12

What are you doing!? Are you crazy?

He knew the answer to that, but he wasn't ready to leave her just yet. He didn't know why, but he had to find out. It had been fifteen minutes since she went upstairs. He hoped everything was okay. The house seemed so peaceful with all the kids in bed. He could definitely get used to this. He heard the soft footsteps of someone coming down the stairs. He hoped she wouldn't be able to see how nervous he was. He was on pins and needles waiting for her to say something. Anything.

He heard her walk up behind him and it took everything not to turn and look at her. "You know, David, I appreciate what you have done tonight and what you are doing now, but I can handle it. I have been for a while now. You don't need to stay."

"If I make you uneasy, I'll go. If I scare you in any way, tell me now and I will leave. I just want to pay you back for your kindness. And maybe spend time with what I hope is a new friend." He still had not turned round. He was half afraid of what he would see and what he would do if he looked at her. He had not been alone with her in eight years. Every time they were in the same room together, someone else was there.

There was silence for a long moment. He heard her walk across the room, open and shut a drawer and then heard her walk his way. She came up beside him on his right and grabbed a dish.

"Thank you again." she said as she dried each dish that he had already washed. "You're a good man, David. I hope you know that."

"I wonder sometimes, but I am glad you think so." He paused for a minute, "I hope I didn't upset the kids too much."

"Why do you think you would upset them?"

He paused for a moment. "Well, the scars."

"I guess they are fine, they never said anything about them. Kids may seem like they only see the surface, but they can be more honest about things than adults. You shared a bit of yourself with them tonight and they may have stopped seeing the scars. I am not sure they have ever really noticed them. They are just a part of who you are to the kids." She paused for a moment, "Did that make sense?"

"Yes, plenty. Wish more adults would do that."

"Me too. They see me with three kids and the looks on their faces goes from happy to pity. Men turn the other way and won't give me a second look."

He thought for a minute about what to say next. Hearing her talk about other men was not on the top of his list. "It was...interesting listening to the banter."

She gave a little "hmm" and said, "That's funny. I thought you were about to bolt out of here like a cat who got his tail stuck in a door." They both looked at each other and had a quick laugh as he nodded in admittance to her observation.

"It has been a long time since I had been around kids so it was a bit noisy for me, but it's okay. It was still good to hear. Can I ask you something personal?"

"Fine but if you get too personal, you're out. Certain secrets are still mine." Emma replied with a chuckle.

"I can agree to that. How long has he been gone? Your husband? I am guessing from Sarah's response that it has been a while."

"Wow, you get right to it don't ya?"

He just responded with a shrug of his shoulder.

She didn't say anything for a while. He figured she was gathering her thoughts on what she was and was not going to say to him. He was curious to hear her answer and was about to apologize for his forwardness when she said, "Eight years. Ryan left us eight years ago." He was watching her while she concentrated on the dish in her hand, maybe over drying it a bit.

"I'm sorry you had to go through that. What do you mean by he left you? Like he died or he packed up and left?" He could see her bottom lip tremble a bit and he wanted to take her in his arms right then and tell her who he really was and what an idiot he had been. Something told him not yet though. So he kept his hands in the water and kept washing. Anything to distract what his instincts told him to do.

"Ryan was in a bad accident eight years ago. I don't know what he was thinking when the tractor hit him, but apparently he was swerving so he didn't hit another car. Funny how that works isn't it. Move to get out of someone's way and you still get hit." She heaved a heavy sigh and he could see the emotions cross her face.

"You don't have to tell me. I am sorry this is so painful for you to talk about. I didn't think. Don't bother saying anything else. Okay?" He put his soapy hand on her arm and her head shot up and she looked him straight in the eye. She was studying him; he could feel it. He didn't like it. She was analyzing him like she used to. Her look had him frozen in his place. He couldn't move. No, he wouldn't move. A part of him was curious to know what she saw or thought.

"No, I need to say it. I have refused to talk about it to anyone who didn't already know." She took a deep breath, "Don't be mad, but can I let the flood gate open and vent? It is usually a girl thing, but..."

He stopped her by saying, "Let it out." He knew he deserved whatever she had to say.

So she did. Boy did she ever. "He refused to see any of his family after a few weeks of being in the hospital. Within three months of the accident, I received divorce papers. It almost killed me. If my friend, Ann, had not stepped in, I would have finished the job he started by sending me those papers. The coward would not answer my calls or see me. He didn't even show up to the hearing. He never fought for me and the kids. Sarah was a newborn. He chickened out for reasons unknown to me or anyone else. The doctor tried to give excuses for him, saying it was trauma. I don't know. I have a hard time with that.

All I know is I was mad at him when he left for work that day and I am mad at him still for leaving us high and dry. He refused to let us see things through after he promised me we would work through everything, because God was on our side." There was a long moment of silence.

She let out her breath like she was relieved. As they stood at the sink, studying one another-awkwardness filling the space between them-her expression changed. She cocked her head to the side a bit, and squinted her eyes and the gasped. He took a step back. He nervously waited for her to say something, but nothing was said. The sound of a cell phone ringing broke the silence.

"Um, is that yours or mine?" He started to bat his pockets, but he knew it wasn't his. *Saved by the bell!*

She picked up her phone, gave another heavy sigh. She seemed to do that a lot. She looked at the caller ID and smiled. She looked happy about whoever was calling.

"Hello?", she answered sweetly. It was like watching a completely different woman. Like changing masks.

"Oh, hi Dr. Emerson... Oh! Okay! This is Mike this time, right?" She gave a little giggle and her smile grew bigger. "No, I wasn't in the middle of anything major. Just washing dinner dishes... Saturday night? Let me see." She looked at the calendar on the wall. "No I do not have anything going this Saturday night...Dinner? I would love to! Yes! I will do all I can to get a sitter...Okay I can do that...Oooo, that sounds nice...Oh that would be fun since I missed last weekend due to Sarah's fall...Oh she is great...Okay, seven o'clock it is…I'm looking forward to it Mike...Thanks for calling...Bye!"

She was just asked on a date. David felt defeated.

He finished the last dish while he assumed she was putting the date on the calendar. He walked to the front door and grabbed his coat and walked out the door without saying goodbye. He did what he said he would do. No more, no less. All he knew now was his Emma was going to go on a date Saturday with a guy she must have liked for her to smile the way she was while talking to him.

That is supposed to be my smile, God.

It was his weekend to work again so he would witness them at the bar. He had a week to figure things out. He could not let her fall for this guy without him getting a chance again. In that moment, he decided he wanted Emma and the kids back and no doctor was going to ruin that chance. Not yet at least.

He was now a man with a mission.

He stopped at his truck and turned to look at the house. He felt an ache in his chest that no matter how hard he tried to ignore, it would not go away. He hated leaving. It felt like home here, like he belonged here.

He got into the truck, never taking his eyes off the house. Just as he turned the key, Emma walked out to the porch and gestured a wave. Her facial expression was asking him if everything was alright. He waved a reply and looked up at the upstairs windows. There, he saw a light on in one with the silhouette of a little girl. She waved to him as well. That sealed it. He was going to figure something out this time. He had to get his family back.

Chapter 13

That night was on Emma's mind all week. She was baffled by the way David left without saying goodbye. She hated that she didn't even get to apologize. She felt terrible for lashing out at him. It wasn't his fault that she had so much built up. She really surprised herself when she let loose like that.

She had gone to the church to look for him. Pastor said he hadn't been in all week. She asked him about who had made the food, so she could thank them, but he said he had no idea what she was talking about. No one had dropped a basket of food off for her family. So that had her mind spinning as well.

She was a little excited about her date with Doctor Mike. He had called her almost every day this week. It was never at a good time, and sometimes he said he was calling to check in on Sarah. She knew better than that. He was a nice man and he had paid extra special attention to Sarah. She just wasn't sure about the timing. She thought she was ready to date again but that old familiar tug to slow down and think had a hold on her. The longing to no longer be alone was a strong emotion and sometimes, it was hard not to give in. She lived by the saying "Listen to your gut first" and it had proven successful. But now she was wondering how much of that was fear and how much was discernment.

So she called up her dear friend, Ann, and asked if she could meet after school for dinner and have a good chat. Ann's husband took her kids so "the moms could get out". She was so thankful to him for doing that. She just hoped and prayed that this night out was not ruined by an accident with the kids again.

***

"So, where to?" Ann asked as she got into Emma's car.

"I want to just have some girl talk and peace. How about Gino's?"

Ann agreed. Emma had a lot on her mind that she had to get off her chest and didn't want a lot of noise and interruptions.

Emma had said all that was on her mind on the drive to the restaurant. It was about a thirty-minute drive, so there was plenty of time to chat. Ann sat, silently, and didn't say a word while Emma rattled on about everything - Dr. Mike, being lonely, how the boys needed a man around and Sarah needed a daddy figure, and how she was tired of waiting. Ann just sat and nodded as an indication that she was listening.

Before the one sided conversation was finished, they arrived at the restaurant. Once orders were placed, they enjoyed lighthearted conversation about life, work and kids. Ann always avoided talking about her marriage with Emma, she didn't want her friend to be hurt more than she already was.

After the dinner plates were taken, and before dessert was brought out, there was a quiet between the two friends. Ann didn't want to say what she felt like she needed to, but she knew she needed to. This was a time to minister to her friend and she was not going to pass it by.

"Emma, have you ever prayed about all the things you told me on the ride here?" Emma fiddled with her silverware, avoiding Ann's stare. Ann could see that she had struck a nerve.

"Ann, I am ashamed to say I have not. I have been so caught up in everything, I guess I forgot." Emma finally admitted.

"Well, as moms and working women, we have a tendency to do that. But I have to ask, why? Are you doing okay? Really? Because from what I see and hear, you sound stressed and kind of bitter. What are you stressed about? Who are you mad at? Really?"

***

Emma sat in silence as she dug deep and looked for an answer. *"Why"* was a good question. She had always had a strong prayer life but she had felt tension and, now that Ann mentioned it, growing bitterness and anger ever since that night in the barn. It just seemed to activate feelings and emotions she thought were long gone. Something about coming home had brought everything back to the front.

Ann's voice broke the silence, "Emma? Honey? Have you ever really dealt with all your feelings about Ryan and the accident? It's not a good idea to get into a relationship when you still hold on to so much from the last one. It isn't fair to the next guy. "

"So what do you suggest? I break the date? I can't do that to him. Not when he is clearly looking forward to it. He has called me every day this week."

"Okay, well take this time then to have a very serious conversation with Dr. Mike about what you are dealing with. He is a doctor, he will understand. I hope. But I would suggest you really pray and evaluate your heart and mind. Take care of things before you move forward too much with any man. And I mean ANY man."

As Emma thought about everything her friend was saying, her throat tightened and her eyes began to burn. Then she felt a tear hit her hand. She felt a churning in her chest and stomach that had nothing to do with the food. She looked up at her friend, through the pool of tears that filled her eyes.

With a whimper, she managed to say,

"You're right...I'm not ready." She looked back at her hands and tightened up her brow. She knew Ann was right, and she knew right where to start. She took a deep breath, wiped her eyes dry and said with determination, "I know right where to start. Can you take me to the site of the accident?"

A smile crept across Ann's face and she stood and said, "Let's go!"

Emma knew it was time for closure, no matter how much it would hurt. Time to stop looking back and letting the past keep her from all that God had in store for her life and the life of her children. No more grieving. It was time to say goodbye.

Chapter 14

Ann offered to keep the kids for the night so Emma could have some quiet and recoup from her emotional night. Ann took her home with a promise to bring the kids and her SUV over as soon as Emma called and told her she was ready. It didn't matter that it might take one night or a whole week, she had told Emma she wanted to see her friend whole again.

She helped Emma to the door and stopped to wait for her to unlock it.

"I've got it." Emma told her with a sleepy smile. "This isn't like it was eight years ago. This is release, not despair. I'll be okay." She took Ann's hand, "Thank you for keeping the kids. You are right, I need sleep and time to think, and as you reminded me, pray." With a hug and a smile, she sent her friend on her way before she turned and walked in the door. She was so glad to have a friend who would give it to her straight but do it so gently that you didn't know you had just been reprimanded.

The house was dark. Emma had forgotten to turn on the porch lights. As she shuffled through the threshold, her foot kicked something that made a crinkling sound. It sounded like a bag of some kind. She stepped over it and turned on the lights. On the floor of her doorway, was a bouquet of varying colored roses. They were beautiful but she was baffled at who would do such a thing. She held the flowers up so she could smell how wonderful they were. The scent filled her heart and made her cry more. She thought she was out all her tears at the accident scene. The fragrance filled her with such warmth and tenderness that she began to feel sleepy. Instead of going to a chair, she just knelt on the floor and sobbed. She hugged the roses like they were a lifeline. She couldn't explain the reason someone would show such an act of kindness, she didn't care. She wasn't even sure she wanted to know who had given them to her. She just hoped that whoever it was would be blessed in return.

Once she could finally get herself off the floor, she shuffled to the kitchen to put the flowers in a vase of water. Her feet and legs tingled and made it hard for her to walk straight. She reached for her favorite vase, one Ryan had gotten for her as a wedding present, and proceeded to fill it. She cut open the packaging and found a little card tucked between the roses. Her hands shook a little with anticipation as she opened the little envelope. She gasped and put her hand to her mouth. The card read:

All is Forgiven

She was shocked. As she studied the card, she went through the list of people in the area who she knew. She didn't think she had wronged any of them. Then it hit her, David. Her behavior the other night was terrible and she felt like a bully for taking out all her anger concerning her husband out on him. She had to find out where he lived. She had to apologize, even though he had clearly forgiven her.

She went to the kitchen and clipped the stems and placed them in the vase. The colors of the antique, mosaic vase blended beautifully with the roses. She decided to take them with her to her room and enjoy them in there. They were for her, and she felt unusually selfish about them. Almost obsessive about not wanting to share their beauty with anyone else in the house. Sometimes, mommies need something just for them.

She was so humbled by his kindness and mentally praised him for having a good eye for something so beautiful. When she reached the sanctuary of her bedroom she closed the door and closed out the world, just for tonight. She searched her room for a place to put the flowers decided right next to the bed would be perfect. That way she could enjoy them first thing in the morning. The intoxicating scent filled her room and for the first time in weeks, Emma took a deep breath and felt herself relax.

She barely had taken off her shoes when she heard the chirp of her phone in her pocket. With a sigh, she looked at the name on the ID and saw it was Dr. Mike. She clicked the answer key and without a greeting, she said, "It has been a long night, I will call in the morning."

With a sound of shock, he said, "That's fine, sleep well and I will talk to you tomorrow."

She turned off the phone and slipped into bed. She paid little attention to putting on her pajamas or washing her face or any of her normal routine. She was checking out for the night and within minutes she was fast asleep.

The next morning, as the sun shone brightly into her room, Emma woke with a smile on her face and a feeling of peace. Once she opened her eyes and saw the roses, she realized the bright colors mirrored what she felt in her heart. Bold, bright, and beautiful. She reached and pulled out the only lavender rose in the bouquet. It was her favorite of all the roses. In fact, she planned to plant a lavender rose bush in the spring right by the porch steps. Its fragrance was so strong, but it didn't overwhelm its admirer. *Maybe I will use this one as a starter. Just have to get it to root.*

Putting the rose back in its place with the rest, she reached for her Bible for the first time in a long time, and began to read in the book of John. When she came to chapter 14 verse 27, she stopped, read it over and over again. It said:

"Peace I leave with you; my peace I give you. I do not give to you as the world gives. Do not let your hearts be troubled and do not be afraid."

It was a promise she knew she could hold onto. God knew what she needed and was going to make sure it happened. In knowing that the timing of what happened the night before was all in His timing and it was one of those Divine appointments she heard another friend talk about. She was going to hold on to this and keep it in her heart.

The peace she felt in her heart had nothing to do with what the world had for her. Not the comfort of her job and whoever was around her but in the healing He had started in her heart the night before and that was more special than anything else the world had to offer her.

With a new spring in her step, she jumped out of the bed and proceeded to get ready for the day. It had been a long time since she felt like the weight of the world was not on her shoulders. It was a beautiful day.

She went to the bedside table and reached for her phone to call Ann. As she waited for it to boot up, she remembered that she had to call Dr. Mike back. She didn't want to break the dear man's heart, but she would, as gently as possible.

As she pushed send, she heard a knock on the front door. While the phone rang, she made her way to the front door. She could see who it was through the glass front door and she was glad that she had gotten herself ready. Mostly, her hair was still up in the towel. She unlocked the door and opened it to the subject of her call. Dr. Mike.

"Well, hello there Sunshine!" he greeted her with a grin that could melt any heart. She hated to make that handsome smile disappear. "I come bearing comfort food and warm drinks for this chilly fall morning. If it is you calling me, I can't answer it right now, but you can leave a message after the beep." His smiled and then said, "beeeep".

The comment and wistful look on his face made her laugh. The fact he brought her food, melted her heart. This was going to be tough. *Do I have to break his heart and turn that gorgeous smile into a frown? It is such a nice smile.* She knew her answer to that. She knew now that she just wasn't ready to date, no matter how much she wanted to get to know this man.

"Come on in, Mike. Sorry I am not completely ready for today but if you don't mind, I don't mind." She opened the door for him and took the bag of goodies he held.

"Not a problem. I know it is early, but you sounded so...spent, and exhausted last night that I thought you would appreciate the surprise. You sounded like you need a friend."

She guided him to the kitchen and began to get plates for whatever was in the bag, and paper towels, just in case it was what she thought it was. "It's fine. I needed to talk to you about the date tonight anyway. First, let's eat! What did you bring to drink?" She was eager to get this over with, but wanted to enjoy his company.

"I don't think I like the sounds of that, but I have a Pumpkin Spice Latte and a JamaicanMe Crazy coffee with no frills."

"I am going to safely guess the latte is for me."

"Please say yes?" He gave her a weary, pleading smile.

"You're right. I hate straight coffee, even if it is slightly flavored. Have a seat."

She peeked inside the bag, and became excited and sad all at once. He even guessed right on her favorite muffin, Blueberry Cheesecake.

"Oh, Mike you're killing me! How did you know this was my favorite?"

"I will admit, I asked the lady at the counter. I knew you were a regular there." He gave her a sheepish, don't-be-mad kind of look.

"It's fine. I am glad you took the time to ask."

She served him his muffin and they began to enjoy the scenery outside and ate in silence.

Then he chimed in.

"Okay, I can't take it. What happened last night? And what is the issue with tonight?"

"First, it is a long story, but just know it was a long night of discovery and healing."

"Healing from what? Are you sick?"

"I had to deal with some things from my past. They were difficult things. Things that hurt in ways I didn't realize. If it had not been for my dear friend, I would have never come to the realization that I was still holding onto a lot of things. That in turn brought me to the realization that..." She paused and let out the breath she was holding, "that I am in no way ready to date. I am sorry Mike, but I just can't. I thought I was ready, but I was too torn and bitter. I still am in a way. I don't want to put you through all that I am dealing with."

"Okay." He sat there for a moment, moved his empty coffee cup around a bit while looking down at the table. With a heavy sigh, he smiled and took her hand. "It's okay, Emma. I had a feeling you were a bit unsure. I can wait. But I do have a request, can we still go to the bar tonight and have a good time, as friends? I like you enough that I don't care what place you hold in my life; I want you in it. Friend or... more than friends. I don't care which one. You are a special person."

She looked at him in amazement. She was stunned. She had expected a completely different response. She wasn't quite sure what, but not this. She smiled at him and shook her head in amazement.

"Please say something?"

"No fancy restaurant, just bar food for dinner tonight. No dressing up, jeans and t-shirts. Friends. Is that what you are saying?"

"Exactly!"

"Then I accept. Oh, but you should know, I don't drink."

"Alright. Then why do you like to go to the bar?"

"Karaoke night and laughter. I get a kick out of watching some of the people and I love to sing. I can get any cocktail without the liquor in it."

"Can I ask if there is a reason you don't drink? Is it a religion thing?"

"Sure, my answer is simple - Stephen, Aaron, and Sarah. They are my main three reasons. Also, I am a control freak and the thought of getting so drunk I lose control does not sit well with me. I have had drinks in the past, but it is a glass of wine. Last time was..." She paused as she thought about it. It hit her like a ton of bricks to the chest. "It was nine years ago. Just before Ryan and I decided to try to have our third baby. Hmmm, I hadn't thought about it in a long time."

They sat in silence for a long time as she remembered the excitement in the choice that she and Ryan had just made. They were ready to welcome another member to the family. Before the memory could really play out in her head, Mike touched her hand and brought her back to the present. She startled and looked him in the eyes.

***

"Yeah, I can see it now, Emma. You need friends more." He just hoped to one day have a woman get a starry, far off look in her eyes when she thought about him. His thoughts on this Ryan guy were nothing he would ever share with her, but the guy better hope they never meet. He wasn't sure he would forget about his oath to preserve life and plummet the guy.

"Okay then. I will be here to pick you up at 6:30? Sound good?"

"Sounds great. And thank you, Mike." She smiled at him and his heart broke a little more. He could already sense the loss his life would have not having her a part of it full time.

They stood and shook hands. "I'll let myself out. You just sit back down and enjoy that muffin and coffee." Once she was seated back in the chair, he bent and kissed to top of her head and then walked out the door.

Chapter 15

He didn't know why he did it, but he had. He had seen the bouquet of roses through the florist's window and it made him think of Emma. *Bold, bright, and beautiful.* He hoped that she enjoyed them. He was going to keep it anonymous, but there was a part of him that wanted her to know. He had a war raging within him since he saw her at Tony's. One side wanted to leave her and the kids be and let them keep moving on without him. They didn't deserve to be tied down to the monster that he saw every time he looked in the mirror.

Then there was the other side. The side that wanted her to see it was him. To see that he missed her. To see that he regretted what he did and felt like a fool for giving up something so wonderful, so beautiful.

Two weeks ago, he stormed into Pastor Cross's office, dropped himself in the chair in front of the desk. The pastor looked at him in surprise. It wasn't their normal meeting day.

"Can I help you?" the pastor asked.

"I can't keep it up, Pastor! I am frustrated and edgy. One minute I am pushing her and the kids away and the next I want to pull them into my arms and tell them the truth. I can't keep up. I try to stay away, but I can't. I drive by their house every day. They are in the church pew in front of me every Sunday. Emma has been coming to the bar I work at with her friends on Saturday nights for karaoke night. Pastor, hearing her sing again drives me mad. I need to have her in my life again but I don't want to burden them with who I am now." David took a breath and was about to keep going on his rant when the pastor stopped him.

"David, the only one keeping you from doing what you know is right and keeping you and your family from being together again, is you. Only you can keep the ball rolling. God brought her and the kids back to town, to stay. Now it is your turn."

He knew the man was right, and he hated it. He hated that he had to humble himself and let her know. There were things that needed to be said. He didn't know how he was going to do it.

"Woo her David. It isn't hard. Leave hints from time to time. That is, if you really want them back in your life," Pastor Cross had added.

So for a week, he moved the idea around in his head, and that was what prompted him to take the food to her house so she didn't have to cook. He was sure she had spent the weekend getting Sarah settled and he knew she would appreciate the gesture. When he saw her pull in the driveway that day, he lost his nerve and told her someone had dropped it off at the church and he was willing to bring it to her. He was right, she did appreciate it. He didn't expect to be asked to stay and share the meal with them. He definitely was not prepared for the tongue lashing he had gotten that he was sure she had no idea she was giving. Knowing that she would feel bad for lashing out at someone, she thought she had just met, would make her feel bad and embarrassed. She was so kindhearted. He knew the flowers and card would let her know that she shouldn't feel bad. He wished he could have seen her reaction when she saw the roses. He knew they were her favorite, especially the lavender one. That was why he asked the florist to put a single one in the bouquet for her. That was his hint. The rest of the roses were in yellows, pinks, reds, and oranges. That single lavender flower was his little way of telling her he thought of her. He was hoping she got the message. He was hoping that the flowers would distract her a bit on her date tonight. He looked at the clock and saw it was 6:45. He knew they would be here in an hour or two, after their dinner portion of the date, too. Clearly the guy didn't know that she was not a "dress up and go out to a nice restaurant" kind of woman. She was jeans and t-shirt, popcorn and a movie or a ride on a Harley through the country side kind of girl. Well at least she was at one time, with him.

He was washing out the mugs, trying to pay attention to the customers at the bar, when a shaft of light came in from the opening door. It was a busy night. Of course this night of the week always was.

His head was bent down, but he heard someone walk up to the bar, "What can I get for ya?" When there was no immediate answer, he looked up, he was staring her in the face. No smile this time. He couldn't imagine what she needed to say that was important enough for her to seek him out on her date.

When she looked over her shoulder, his eyes followed her glance. At a table in the corner sat who he assumed was the Doctor. She turned back to him with a sheepish smile.

"Hi David."

"Good evening Emma. What can I get for you and your friend?"

"Oh the waitress has already taken our order. I was wondering if you had a second? If not that's okay. I just wanted to talk to you real quick."

"Are you sure he won't mind?" he gestured with his head. "The only quiet place, on a night like tonight, is in the back alley."

"Sure, I already told him I had to talk to you, but I should let him know where I will be. Come on and I will introduce you." He looked to his left and Eddie, the other bartender, was chatting it up with a pretty, half-dressed woman at the end of the bar.

"Hey, lover boy, I'm taking a quick break. Watch the bar for me." He yelled over the music. He got a kick out of making Eddie turn red. Anger or embarrassment, he really didn't care why the punk turned red. David just enjoyed getting a rise out of the guy.

"Lead the way." He made a gesture toward the table.

She grabbed his hand when he came around the bar and dragged him to the corner table. He wouldn't lie and say he didn't enjoy having her hand in his again, even for a minute.

The doctor looked him up and down and then stared him in the eye. *Is he sizing me up?* He began to walk a little straighter and puff his chest out a little more, leaning less on his cane. He need it to due to arthritis being bad tonight but he was not about to let the doctor know it. He slipped a lazy grin on his face as they approached. He saw the man's face change from uncertainty to a look of pity then to a look of terror. *I know I'm scary, so be scared buddy!*

The good doctor stood and shook David's hand. As they shook hands the doctor's eyes grew wide as he noticed more of the scarring and clearly felt the burns on David's hand.

"Nice to meet you, I'm Mike." he said.

"David."

"Mike, we are going to step out back for a minute, you good for a bit? I promise I won't be long."

Emma let go of his hand and placed it on Mike's in an affectionate way. It made David's muscles tighten which made the grip of the handshake get a little stronger. *She was mine first, buddy.* He was sure the man was getting the hint. The wince that quickly dashed across the man face told him he had.

He finally let go of his hand. The doctor was rubbing his hands together like he was rubbing off the pain David just inflicted.

"Um, yeah, sure. I'll just hold down the table."

"Great! Thanks for understanding." She turned to him now, "Okay let's go."

He took her through the kitchen and out the back door. It was a little creepy, but it was quiet. He held the door open for her and as she walked by him, he caught the scent of her perfume. The kind he had bought for her every year for their anniversary. It took a lot of willpower to not take her in his arms right then but he didn't because he didn't want to scare her. He had to remember that he was just a stranger to her. Someone she had just met a few weeks ago. The look of her in the moonlight was enough for him to want to throw all his plans out the window and completely and totally give in. *Okay God, I give in. Show me what to do. Tell me what to say and pave the way. If this is what you want, then make it happen.*

"So what's on your mind, Emma?"

"Well first, I want to say thank you. Thank you for bringing the food. It was a wonderful meal. Where did you learn to cook like that?"

"Well, my mom taught me...wait, how did you know it was me?" *Nice one Daniels! You walked right into that one.*

"I went and asked Pastor Cross. He said no one had said anything about a meal to him or brought one in. No one even knew yet that there was an accident. So you were my only other guess. My parents would have just come over. It wasn't hard really." She gave him a curious look, then asked, "How did you know?"

"Well, um. One of the nurses?" He could feel his palms sweat. He hunched over a bit and put much of his wait on his cane. He was trying to look cool and relaxed. "I had to do repairs at her place."

"I don't believe you, because there is this thing called HIPAA and she could lose her job. But right now, I am not worried about it. I still know it was you."

"You're good. Like a detective. Observant, smart." *And beautiful as ever.* He gave her a lazy smile.

"Yeah, well, when you have two boys who don't say much, you have to know how see between the lines and ask the right questions.

I also want to apologize. I lashed out at you and you had nothing to do with my problems.

You didn't deserve it and I am sorry. I know you have forgiven me, thank you for the roses as well, but I feel like I should still ask." She stopped, tilted her head to one side and studied his face. It was like she was asking a million questions without saying a word. He hated it when she would do that. Analyzing, that is what she called it one time. They stood in the alley for what felt like forever. The only sounds were the cars driving by and the faint sound of thumping from the bar. Or was it his heart pounding in his chest?

While he was fixated on her eyes, he was to caught in her eyes to see her hand come to his face. He touch was soft and stirred longing for more with in him. Her ever studying gaze locked him in place and he watched as a flood of questions flashed over her face. What was it he was seeing in her eyes? Did she feel what he was feeling? Could she see in his eyes everything he wanted to say? He was so mesmerized by her, that he forgot about all that was going on around them. He forgot the years of being apart. His mouth went dry with his next thought.

I wonder if her lips are still as sweet as they were before. Their faces where so close because of the way he was leaning on his cane but her voice broke the spell he was under.

"David, you are a puzzle, but I find myself wanting to figure it out." Her voice was just a whisper. Like a light, refreshing breeze on his face. He couldn't take this. It was all or nothing. He had to tell her and be done with it.

"Emma, there is something…"

"Hey Dave! You coming back in or what? We are getting slammed in here." *I am going to ring that punk's neck after work.*

"I have to go," he whispered. "Can I come by tomorrow and we can talk then?" Her eyes were no longer soft and penetrating, but startled. He wasn't sure what changed, but he was needed inside. He would have to find out later.

"Yeah, sure. I'd like that." Her words sounded strained and confused, like she…*Oh forget it David, get to work.*

With an agitated sigh, he swung the back door open and held it for her, but she didn't move. "I will go around front; I suddenly don't feel well. I just need some air for a moment and I will be in. Thank you." She walked to the corner of the building and disappeared.

***

Emma's head was spinning. She didn't know if it was from the smells in the air of the alley or the contact she had with David. She knew in her heart what it was, but she didn't want to let herself believe it. She didn't want to believe that she was drawn to him. He mesmerized her and confused her all at one. There was something about the glimmer in his good eye that almost made her think...*No! It can't be. Could it God?* He was the only other man she had felt that draw to, that earth shattering connection with. Because of his scars, he looked nothing like Ryan but the spark of electricity she just felt between them had her second guessing herself. She had an unusual desire to kiss the man, just to figure it out.

She let out a long breath. She couldn't get her mind to quit spinning. "Oh get it together girl!" she said to herself. She took another deep breath, shook her hands in hopes to shake out the electric burn she still felt. It had sent shivers down her spine. Awareness, that this wasn't just some man but maybe someone more special.

A couple more deep breaths and she turned for the door and went inside. As she passed the bar, she couldn't keep her eyes from drifting in David's direction. When she looked his way, she saw he was looking right back at her. Again, she was so fixed on him that she ran right into someone. That shook her right out of her daze. When she looked up at who she walked into, she noticed it was Mike. She could tell he was truly concerned for her. His hands were on her arms trying to stabilize her. She hoped that she would feel something like she felt with David, but nothing. Just a friend who was looking out for her.

He looked from her to David and back again, "Everything okay, Emma? Did he say or do something to you? You are as white as a sheet."

She could see the concern in his eyes, but she could also see a hint of jealousy. She had come here with him, and spent most of the time in the alley with David. Innocent as it was, she couldn't blame him. He was really going to be upset with her request because she couldn't stay here anymore. She wanted to go home, put on her soft pajamas and curl up in a blanket. She did not want to think or feel right now.

"I am alright, but I would like to go home now. I am sorry, but I really want to go, now." Her mind raced for something to say. "I'm not feeling well." She hoped that would get his focus off David.

"Alright, if you're sure." He escorted her out the door and she caught him cast a glare at David overhead as they walked past him, but she could feel David's gaze was squarely on her.

The drive home was a quiet one. While she looked out the passenger side window, she could see Mike's reflection in the glass. He kept glancing her way. She knew that she should feel bad about cutting her date short, but honestly, she didn't. She had more important things going on in her head right now. To justify it, she told herself that she would be too distracted to be good company.

She needed to say something. You could cut the tension with a knife.

"I really am sorry, Mike. I would completely understand if you never want to see me again. I won't even hold it against you if you want to refer Sarah's case to another doctor."

He didn't respond until he pulled into her driveway. He very abruptly put the car into park and turned off the car. She was waiting for a bad reaction when he turned in his seat and looked at her. She could see all the questions he had swirling in his eyes like a whirlpool.

He reached over the center console and took her hand in his. "Are you sure you're okay? You looked pretty spooked when you came into the bar. If he did something to you, if he laid a finger on you in a way that was unwanted, I will go back to that bar and take care of him..."

Though his protectiveness was endearing, she had to stop him, "NO! No, he didn't touch me, at all, in any way. Not a finger. Please stop those thoughts now. He did nothing wrong. It was just..." She didn't want to say what was going through her mind right now. She was afraid to admit out loud what she felt in her heart. She was too confused.

"Emma, it was just what? We have established that this is a friendship, so I am not mad about the way he looked at you, but at the fact you looked terrified. Talk to me, like I was one of your girlfriends. Close your eyes and picture your best friend if you have to."

Well that was a thought. She knew she would not be able to sort this out without vocalizing it even if it did scare her. What could it hurt? So she closed her eyes and she tried to picture her best friend. The one person she could tell anything to. The face that came to mind pierced her heart. He had been her best friend. There were no secrets between them. It was Ryan. That's when she felt a finger touch her cheek to wipe away a tear she had no idea she had shed.

Her eyes flew open in time to see Mike pull his hand away. He grabbed a handkerchief out of his pocket and handed it to her. "I promise, it is unused. I just have a need to always have one handy." He gave her a partial smile, "Go ahead and take it. Please, dry your eyes, because I can't stand seeing a woman cry. It makes me want to do things that are not very gentlemanly. I don't want to do that. So hurry up." She wiped her eyes with a giggle and looked back at him.

"I can't do what you suggest. My best friend was Ryan. We told each other everything. There were no secrets between us."

"Ryan? That is your ex, right?" Emma had never referred to him as her "ex". It just didn't seem to fit. She hated the sound of it. Like the relationship was finished.

"Yes, he was my husband. We were married for six years when he had his accident and we were together for four years before then. We had

had a powerful connection right away. I felt it the day he finally found his courage to talk to me. I could feel his presence just before he entered a room. My parents thought I was overly dramatic as a teen when I told them that. My friends thought it was all in my head but I knew. I just knew. It was like, oh how do I put this? Before, I felt good about myself and life and what not, but there was always something missing. I was a strong Christian in high school, and I had a good relationship with the Lord, but there was still a piece of the life puzzle that I hadn't found it yet. I wasn't looking but I knew it was coming too.

When he came and sat behind me that day in history class and we started to talk, I immediately felt a sense of completion. Like I had found that other piece of the puzzle. Does that make any sense to you?"

She could tell he was rolling the idea around in his head. "So you are saying he was your soul-mate? Your better half."

"Not my better half, just my other half. Well, when he refused to see me while he was still in the hospital recovering, I thought I was dying. When he sent me the divorce papers, I went over the edge. I was lost. I lived in blackness until my friend came over to the house and made me see that I couldn't stop living because I had three children who needed me. I had to keep going. If for no one else then I had to live for them. So, after a lot of prayer and counseling, I signed the papers and moved on." She need a breath; this next part is what scared her. "I just moved back to town, Mike. I haven't been home in a long time. The memories here are good and bad, they bring joy and heartache. I haven't seen Ryan since the afternoon of the accident. I have no clue what he looks like without the bandages. He suffered massive burns and scarring on his face. He practically shattered his right leg. He can't look the way he did when we first met. Right? I mean, scars like he must have would change a person completely, right?" She was looking for some kind of reassurance or confirmation.

"It would make a person unrecognizable if they are as bad as you say. Do you know his reason for turning you away? I mean if you were as close as you say you were, then why would he let go of that? I know I wouldn't."

"I don't know. Here is what has me spooked, Mike. When I first met David, there was something about him that was familiar to me. I couldn't put my finger on it. I felt as if I had known him. The same thing happened the day of Sarah's appointment. I came home, and he was sitting in his truck, right here in the drive, with a cooler full of food for the kids and me. He said someone dropped it off at the church. So tonight, I had to say something to him. I had told you that I behaved badly toward him that night. When we were standing out in the alley, talking, I was watching him, studying him. He looked so sad and something came over me and I touched his face, and BAM! That old feeling hit me, like a lightning bolt. What I am getting at, and I am scared to admit, is... oh I don't know if I want this or not Mike?"

He squeezed her hand. He was still holding it. "Emma, you can't move forward if you don't acknowledge your past."

"But then it's real and then I have to deal with it. I don't want to. I just faced the accident scene last night. This is too soon. I don't know how I feel about what he did."

"EMMA! Quit over thinking it and just tell me what you think."

"I think David is...is...I think he might be Ryan!" Then the dam that held back her tears broke open and a flood poured from her eyes.

Angry tears, happy tears, confused tears, healing tears.

Mike reached over and wrapped his arm around her shoulders. He sat there and held her for a good twenty minutes. She took a deep breath and looked at Mike. He was being such a sport about this. He could have pushed her out the car door when they pulled in and left her sitting in the gravel. But he didn't. He encouraged her. He held her hand through her ramble and helped her admit to what she feared.

"I am so sorry for dumping my drama on you like that. Here you were hoping to be more than friends and I tell you about my feelings about another man. I am so inconsiderate. I..."

"Stop right there. How do you know that a part of me isn't holding out, hoping you will keep him on the curb and fall into my arms?" He gave her a raised eyebrow and a cockeyed grin. It made her laugh a little. "There, I guess my job is done for the night. Don't worry. I will bill your insurance for this house call."

"Oh stop it." She gave him a grin with a roll of the eyes and shook her head at his attempt to make her feel better. "Thank you Mike for letting me unload. It would have kept me up all night. It might still."

"As long as my new friend feels better. Do you, Emma?"

"I do but I don't. I'll get to the bottom of this." She looked at his watch and saw how late it was. "Oh wow! It is late, or early. I have church in five hours and a possible ghost from my past to face. Thank you again and maybe we can try this again another time." She opened the car door to get out. She looked back in, "Thank you again. It certainly sealed the friendship for me."

With a wave of the hand, she shut the door on the car and climbed the porch steps. She had a long night and day ahead of her. God, I need a clear head and strong heart to face what is in front of me now. Help me see what you want me to see. If it is him, help me to deal with all these emotions.

She didn't bother to turn lights on in the house, she just felt her way up the stairs stumbled into her room, and fell into her bed. The last thing she saw in the moonlight were the roses David had given her.

Chapter 16

He had been looking for her since he arrived at church twenty minutes ago. She looked so...spooked when she left last night. He had an aching need to talk to her. He had to know if she was okay. *Oh face it, you want to know if she knows.* He knew keeping this secret was not good, but he just wasn't ready yet. He wanted her to know on his terms.

"God's time is not our time" Pastor Cross' words rang through his head. He knew in his heart that he was not really in control of this whole situation. He had tried things his way and had regretted it. He had not had a night of peace in the last eight years. He kicked himself every time he saw her walk down the street or drove by her house.

The service had started and she still had not arrived. She was too punctual to be late. He tried his best to focus on the music and announcements, but it just was not happening.

At that moment, the church door swung open and the cool November breeze came through the sanctuary doors. He could have sworn he had caught a slight scent in the air of her perfume. His mind apologized to God for the sudden racing of his heart but he couldn't help it. She still felt like a part of him, even if they were apart. *"What God has brought together, no man, not even I, can tear apart."* *Is that what you are reminding me God?*

He sat in the back of the sanctuary as always, so he glanced back and saw her struggling again the fall wind close the heavy outside door. Just as he was about to go help her, an usher stepped up and together they closed the door. As she turned to enter the sanctuary, her eyes locked right on his. He could always tell what she was thinking by looking into her eyes. She let him know what was on her mind through her eyes, even when she wasn't aware of it. Like right now, her eyes were saying, "I am confused." Seeing that made his heart hurt. He had a suspicion of what she felt between them last night. He had the advantage though of knowing who she was. She was not so fortunate. The electricity that moved through him last night was the same as the night he took the food to her house. He didn't want to think too inappropriately in church, but he knew what it was. It was that part of him that only she could bring to life because she was his first and only. He had never known any other touch but hers, and it set off all kinds of bells. He quickly turned to focus on what was going on at the front of the congregation. This line of thinking was going to get him in trouble. He saw her walk past him out of the corner of his eye. As she passed, his attention was back on her. *Okay man, that's enough. You're in church!* He scolded himself with a slight grin. He snapped his eyes away from where they had wandered and took a glimpse around the room to see if anyone caught him watching her walk away. It looked like he was in the clear, until he glanced up at Pastor Cross, sitting in a chair just behind the podium while someone gave announcements. They locked eyes and then Pastor grinned and shook his head. David knew he had been caught and it would be something they would talk about tomorrow. He felt like a kid who got his hand caught in the candy jar by a very angry mama. He could feel the heat of embarrassment creep up his neck and warm his ears and face. He knew he should be ashamed, but if he was honest, he really wasn't. She was his wife at one time.

***

At the end of the sermon, Ann came and greeted Emma while her husband went to the classrooms to get the kids. They stood off to the side and chatted for a minute.

"Well, you sure were late today. Everything okay?"

Emma gave a heavy sigh, "Yeah, just a lot on my mind."

"Anything you want to talk about?"

"Not today. I think I need to just pray about this one. I think God is showing me something and I am not sure I am ready to see it. So, just be praying for me. Lord knows I need all the prayers I can get right now."

Ann put her hands on Emma's shoulders, dipped her head down with closed eyes, and began to pray. Emma followed her lead. She prayed that God would guide Emma's footsteps and her heart. That He would reveal in His time all he wanted her to see. She said a few more words that Emma didn't hear because she suddenly became very distracted by some one's presence, and then she heard her friend say "Amen". They both looked up at the same time and looked at each other, but as Emma looked at Ann to say "thank you", she saw David over her friend's shoulder and felt the blood drain from her face.

"Emma?" she heard Ann call her and then turned her head to see what had her attention. When she turned back, she asked, "Does he bother you?"

"What? No! Just something about him. I hate that I can't figure it out."

"Maybe you are not supposed to figure it out and maybe you are supposed to just let God work. He can't show you anything if you keep getting in His way. Just relax, and quit your analyzing."

"You know, you're right. I am over thinking it. I am doing what I have always done and it isn't always a good thing. Thank you Ann." The two women embraced as they were rushed by children.

"I will talk to you later. I guess it is time to take this crew home." With a wave, Ann and her family were headed for the door.

Just as she turned to her own crew of hungry children, she saw David walk toward them. She didn't think she was ready to talk to him again, but it could not be avoided. She could hear the kids vying for her attention, but couldn't make out what they were saying. She was so nervous that her ears were ringing. Finally, Sarah tugged on Emma's arm.

"What is it honey?"

"Can we go now? I'm hungry."

"Yes." She got the car keys out of her purse and handed them to Stephen, "Go ahead and get the car warmed up. You all head to the car. I'll be right there. I need to talk to one more person."

"Aww, Mom, you always say 'really quick' and it ends up being an hour." Aaron was acting like a five-year-old, a sassy five-year-old.

"GO! NOW!" She said in a stern but quiet voice. She could feel her eyes bulge in an attempt to stress her level of irritation.

They all left with grumbling and complaining to be heard by all. She figured they did not sleep well by the way they were behaving.

As soon as they were outside, she caught movement out of the corner of her eye. She knew it was him. Uncertain if it was nerves of the possibility or something else altogether, but her stomach started to flutter and a feeling of giddiness swelled inside her

"Hi," was all she could manage at the moment.

He was first watching the kids walk out the door, but when she spoke, he looked down at her with a smile, "Hi. Are they always like that, or just today?" Was he poking fun at her? The thought made her smile back and the fluttering increase. Ryan could always get the butterflies going. *What does it mean that David is doing the same? This isn't the same as nervousness.*

"No, that is a normal thing, especially if they are tired." She turned her whole body to look at him full on. Something she learned years ago to do when you want to give someone your full attention. "So, Mr. David, did you enjoy the sermon?"

"What I caught of it." He was now looking at her with such intensity it made her begin to feel a little warm. She noticed his Adam's apple bounce a little. *He feels it too!* "I was a bit distracted today which made it hard to focus on what was being said. I meet with Pastor every Monday morning anyway, so I will hear it again."

"Oh okay." Awkward pause, she didn't know what else to say but she wanted to know more, to know if her suspicions were right. "So what are you doing for supper, Mr. David?"

"Just call me David. No 'Mr.' is necessary. I'll probably head home and have a sandwich, tend to my animals, watch some football."

"Oh well...How does barbecue chicken sound? I have plenty for one more person. You are welcome to join us." Emma didn't know what possessed her to ask him to dinner, but she figured it would give her a chance to get to know the man, and maybe even have a few questions answered.

"I like barbecue chicken. It's one of my favorites. Just let me run home and tend my animals and get some jeans on and I will be right over. I can't stand being dressed up like this much longer." His comment made her laugh and broke the tension.

"Sure sounds good. Will an hour give you enough time?"

"Plenty. See you soon."

They walked out the doors, almost together. Out of the corner of her eye, she caught Pastor slap David on the back, shake his hand, give him a knowing smile and a nod. She had a feeling they just had a conversation without words. It made her smile. *Even if he isn't Ryan, he still seems like a good man.*

Chapter 17

He hoped this wasn't a bad idea, but she had tempted him with his favorite meal. It had been a long time since he had barbecue chicken and even longer since it was hers. His decision was strictly made by his stomach, but the idea of having a Sunday dinner with them had its own appeal. He would get to know his kids, see what they are into and if he arrived early enough, he would get to watch her cook. It always amazed him when he watched her toss, stir and cut. It was like a maestro directing an orchestra. It was beautiful.

He pulled into the drive and saw kids running around in the side yard. They were laughing and playing. Sarah was on a tire swing as her brothers pushed her from each side. She had hooked her good hand around the swing and it looked like the boys were being careful. It made him smile to see them like this, but it hurt too. It hit him that if he had stayed, their life would have been so much more than they had now. Oh the lessons he had learned over the last eight years. He kicked himself every morning for giving up his family. A part of him still thought they deserved better than what he had to offer, but he also knew there were certain things you could only learn from your dad.

He parked his truck next to her red SUV. He smiled remembering that day he watched her drive by the church and had the feeling it was her. He was right. He got out of the truck and waved back at the kids as they hollered at him, "Hi!".

He had to smile at their energy considering how they were behaving after church. He figured she must have kicked them out of the house for a while. That thought made him smile because he then imagined what he would do if they were still married. He would be pestering her with kisses while she tried to get things ready, demanding her attention.

He stopped at one the steps, looked at the door, then at the kids, then back to the door. He wondered if going inside would be a good idea. He would be alone with her and he had been having a bit of a hard time remembering they were not married when he saw her earlier. Even last night in the alley, he almost pulled her in his arms to kiss her like he had wanted to since he first seen her in the pizzeria.

"Lord, here I am again. Keep me strong. Just because we were once married, doesn't mean I can act like we still are. Help me respect her." With that little prayer sent from his mouth to God's ears, he approached the door and knocked.

No answer. He knocked again. Then he heard music booming from the back of the house. It was a fun tune that had a funky beat. He imagined her in the kitchen dancing as she prepared the meal.

She was a great dancer, but only he had ever seen her. He checked the door and saw it was not latched, so he went in. Sure enough, he was greeted with a loud hip hop tune from their younger days. He followed the sound to the kitchen where he couldn't help but smile at what he saw. He guessed right, she was dancing. He crossed his arms, leaned against the door frame and just watched her. He knew any minute she would break out singing, which was always the next step. She must have been feeling nostalgic because it was a song that was played at their wedding reception. She had played it many times while cooking and broke out into dance when she thought no one was looking. He missed this. He decided then and there that he would do his best to win her back, but he would take it slow.

***

The kids had pushed their limit on the ride home so she told them they were not allowed in the house while she cooked supper. When they got home, they changed into their play clothes and she pushed them outside. She needed to relax a bit before David arrived. She had found an old song from her high school years and proceeded to dance in the kitchen. She had cranked the volume and got lost in the song. She was starting to actually enjoy herself. She was about to break out into song when she felt someone watching her and turned.

She squealed like a school girl at the sight of him leaning on the door frame of her kitchen. She hadn't heard him knock. She felt the heat of embarrassment rise up her neck and cover her cheeks. He had a lazy smile on his face that made his eyes dance in a mischievous way.

"Enjoy the show, David?"

"Sure. Didn't realize there was a show to go with dinner. Where can I buy tickets? I think it is worth seeing again."

They both started laughing as she went to turn off the song.

"How much of that did you see?"

"Oh enough. Enough to know you like to dance and do it often."

"Well, since you intruded on my cooking routine, you can make the salad. Tomatoes, lettuce, cucumbers and sunflower seeds are there on the counter. Start chopping." She was going to make him pay. "And if word gets around town what you saw, you are a dead man."

They were still laughing about it when he said, "If this is a daily thing, I'll be back tomorrow." She caught the hint of flirtation in his tone. She glanced at him out the corner of her eye and caught the hint of a smile. He was smiling and laughing, but his eyes told her he meant it. She found it unnerving that she enjoyed the looks he gave her. For some reason, it felt right having him here in her kitchen, in her home. It was like he belonged there.

Watching him chop the veggies made her think of the last time she and Ryan worked together in the kitchen preparing Sunday supper. David made her think of Ryan even more now that she saw how he was moving and cutting. *Don't fall for him Emma. Not until you know.*

"So, Emma, tell me what you do for a living?" His question shook her out of her thoughts.

"I am a history teacher at the high school. This is my first year."

"Were you teaching before you moved here?"

"I taught at an elementary school in Ohio right after college. When this position opened up, I did all I could to get back home."

"So you grew up here?"

"Yup, just on the other side of town. It was hard leaving my parents and family behind, but I knew I would be back someday. I am glad it was sooner rather than later. Of course, all my family has left town, but my friends are still here and they are like family to me." She worried for a moment that maybe she was giving a lot of information but she felt comfortable talking to him. "So how about you? You said you are from here as well?"

"Yeah. I have been gone for quite a while as well. I know what you mean about coming home."

"What did you do while you were away? Why did you leave?" She hoped that he would not see through her questioning. She had to know what happened.

"Well, I traveled from town to town. Doing odd jobs, kind of like I do here."

"So are you just passing through? Or are you here to stay?"

"I'm not sure yet. It all depends. But I hope I am here to stay. It is nice being home again."

"Does your family live around here?"

"No, but I have seen my sister around town."

"You mean you have been here for a year and you have only seen your sister? Why?"

All flirting and funny business had left his tone. The knife in his hand stilled and she watched as his chest rose and fell. "Have you looked at me lately? I am a real life monster. I have nieces and nephews who would be horrified."

"Why would you think that? My kids don't shy away from you. I am not sure they even see your scars. Well, I know Sarah does, but she doesn't miss details and is very compassionate and perceptive. She sees the heart of a person."

"She must get that from her mother." She had stopped brushing the sauce on the chicken and looked at him. He was watching her. She couldn't tell what he was looking for, but he was searching her this time.

"Why did you leave David?"

"Why do you want to know?"

"Understanding. Clarity."

"Because of your husband?"

"Yeah, in a way. You said you had a family at one time. Why did you leave?"

Just as he was about to answer her, the kids came thundering in and all conversation stopped. She moved to put plates on the table when he caught her by the arm. Her eyes were wide with surprise and wonder. She could hear a faint rattle of the plates in her hands. She was shaking. Did she make him as nervous as he made her?

"Can we talk about it later? It isn't exactly dinner conversation."

She was breathing a little faster than before.

"We can talk later. That would be good."

***

He had hoped they could talk after dinner, but the kids were really rambunctious today, so he decided it was best to go shortly after dinner.

Emma walked him out to his truck, "You don't have to leave. Kids are just being kids." Her somewhat pleading tone made him wonder if she wanted him to stay.

"No, I think maybe it is best. They seem like they are wound up pretty tight. I can come by another time, if you would like." He hoped she would be alright with that.

He could hear the gears of indecision turning in her pretty little head. "That would be fine. Maybe next weekend. I am super busy during the week with school."

"Sounds great. I'll see ya later."

He stood there a moment more, not really wanting to leave, but knew he had to. She didn't move back to the house right away either. He wondered what she was thinking. For a change, her face wasn't giving away too much information.

"Yeah, I'll see ya later." He made the move first to get in the truck. Then she finally moved toward the house.

He pulled out of her driveway and made his way home. As he was leaving, he was distracted by the events of the afternoon and Emma's behavior. It was like they were kids again and no one wanted to leave the other's presence. Looking back at what they once had would do him no good though. It was only the future from here. God brought them back to town. He had to do his part now. This was his chance.

Chapter 18

The next three Sunday afternoons, David joined them for dinner. Everyone got along so well that there was just a natural flow. The kids seemed glad to have him around. The scars that to some might be repulsive, seemed to not bother the kids. When they talked at the table, they all looked right at him like nothing was different from the next guy.

For Emma, though, it was nice having an adult male around. Someone to talk with, to ask about guy things so that she had a better idea what was coming with the boys. After dinner, the kids would do dishes while they would walk to the pond and talk about family, work, God – whatever was on their minds. Even though all the leaves were gone and the temperatures were dropping drastically, it didn't seem to stop their walks. They just added layers. It wasn't like talking with Ann or Tiffany, all the giggling and tee-heeing, but deep, meaningful conversations. There had been some teasing and joking. Emma had discovered that David actually had a great sense of humor.

By week three, she had begun to look forward to having him over. Having a man around the house, even if it is only on Sunday, brought her a feeling of contentment. Last night, she had even let herself begin to think that maybe this was leading into something else. The wonder of his true identity had taken a back seat to everything else going on in their budding friendship.

So today, the Sunday before Thanksgiving, they had continued with their weekly routine and set out the back door. The snow had not fallen yet, but you could feel it in the air. They were bundled from head to toe. Long Johns, sweaters, thick jeans, heavy winter coats, gloves, and sock hats. Emma even had a scarf on, and David had a Thermos full of hot cocoa in one hand and his cane in the other.

"You know, David," she started with a smile on her face "we are going to have to stop with these walks before too long. The weatherman is calling for the snow to start this week. I am not sure I will be able to keep from freezing to death. I worry that you'll slip on the ice."

"Oh, I don't know about that. I could always lean on you instead of using the cane, and we can still add more layers." He looked at her with a flirty grin and she felt like someone just turned up the heat.

"I am not sure I can support you. It's not like you're a small guy."

"Hmm, well let's see." He handed her his cane and the Thermos and wrapped his arm around her and leaned on her a bit. She was not ready for it in any way and they both fell to the ground. They broke out in hearty laughs that echoed over the frozen woodland.

"I told you it wouldn't work. You're a big ol' beast of a man. My five-foot-three, one hundred forty-five-pound stature can't take your six-foot three, two hundred twenty-pound frame. Now get off!" Neither of them could control their laughter. They fumbled and laughed so hard that David lost his balance and fell. In trying to stay on his feet, he grabbed hold of Emma, but instead of her steadying him, he took her down with him. Both of them sat on the ground until they could settle down enough to get up and walk. Even though the cold of the ground was creeping up through her bones, she couldn't bring herself to get up. She began to feel that odd little flutter again when they locked eyes and instantly stopped laughing. She felt frozen in place and it had little to do with the weather.

She was caught off guard that this man could make her feel something that no other man could, except one. And if she was honest with herself, she didn't care that it wasn't Ryan.

She felt her head start to spin a bit and she began to breathe a little more rapidly. *What do I do now?*

***

They were having a great time. He felt like he had gotten her to loosen up a bit and they were just enjoying one another's company. That was until they locked eyes and her face changed. She wasn't smiling anymore. She actually had a look of panic. He couldn't figure out what had changed. *Unless...Is it possible? Could she learn to love me as David?* He wasn't sure what to do, but he took hold of the opportunity, and her hand.

"Emma? You okay? Did you hurt something? Did I do something?"

As she was starting to breathe rapidly, he could see the puffs of white coming from her mouth in quick succession. *Oh that mouth. It sure wouldn't take much...* but he hesitated too long though and just as he began to lean in, she rose to her feet tugging him up with her.

"Are you okay Emma?" He asked as he stood.

"Yeah, I think so." She looked a little bewildered now.

He stepped forward a bit and touched her face with his gloved hand. Looking deep into the icy blue pools of her eyes, he could see the wheels turning. "Oh what I would give to know what you are thinking right now." He let a slow grin creep across his face, "Care to enlighten me?"

***

NO! No, I am not ready to enlighten you.

The fear she churning within her playing out scenarios in her head about Ryan seeing her in the arms of another man. Then it hit her that if Ryan was going to come back, he would have by now.

She needed space and time to think, so she took a step back and made up an excuse to end the walk.

"I-I think I hurt my ankle a bit, let's head back." She turned to walk back to the house and he grabbed her arm and pulled her back to him.

"Only if there isn't anything else you want to share with me." His look was serious. So she challenged him a bit and gave him her "stern mom" stare.

"I am sure. I am freezing now and I need to ice my ankle." *Nice cover girl. Now make it believable.* She began to limp ever so slightly as they made their way back to the house.

Along the way, she had a thought cross her mind to distract her from what was happening between them.

"Where are you going for Thanksgiving?"

"Nowhere, I suppose. Just me, the game and a Hungry Man TV dinner." He sounded frustrated.

She came to an abrupt halt and turned on him, "Oh I don't think so Buddy. You're coming here."

He straightened his shoulders and looked her square in the face, "And what if I don't want to? You gonna make me, shorty?"

"Well," she popped a hip out and waved her hand like she didn't care, "if you are happy with fake food, stay home. But here, you will get the full dinner, fresh from the oven. Your choice," she softened up a bit, "but it would be really nice if you would come."

She could tell she had just disarmed him as his shoulders began to relax a bit. A smile crept across his face and he reached for her hand and ran his thumb ever so lightly over the back of her hand. She felt her heart begin to race. She could feel it right through her glove.

"Emma, I would love to join you for dinner." The smile that was on his lips left with a thought. "Is your dad going to be there? I don't think he likes me much."

She laughed at that. "No, my parents are visiting an aunt in Florida. You will be safe. What was up with that, anyway?"

He never answered her and instead walked her to the back door of the house, kissed her gloved hand, and said, "Good night Emma." Then he walked away without waiting for her response.

Okay, I guess he'll let me know when he is ready.

Chapter 19

Thanksgiving morning, Emma felt like she was running a marathon. She was ready to scream at the next person who talked to her. The boys were fighting over the TV. Sarah was up in her room crying because Aaron said something mean to her. The dog was out back barking into the woods. She figured there was an animal out there taunting him. She thought about calling David and telling him to bring all his Hungry Man TV dinners because she was in no way ready to make a big meal.

She could still hear the boys in the living room fighting when she lost it. Enough was enough. She took a deep breath, cleaned her hands which were covered in egg, bread crumbs and seasonings, and walked to the living room.

"If you two are not going to stop fighting, then go to your rooms. I am done listening to the fighting. Go or you are grounded for life!"

They did as they were told but fought all the way up the stairs to their bedrooms. She knew they had reached their doors because they each slammed them. The vibration knocked a picture off the wall in the hall and broke the glass.

"Great, one more thing to do." She picked it up while trying to think of a way to make the boys replace it. When she turned it over and looked at the picture, her heart sank. It was one of her and Ryan on the day of their wedding. She felt the air in her lungs leave her chest and knelt on the floor, no longer caring about the dinner or the kids. All she could see was his face.

He was such a handsome man. His dark sable colored hair was glistening in the picture. His hazel eyes danced as he looked down at her. It was a picture of the two of them gazing lovingly into one another's eyes. Their facial expressions showed what they were feeling inside. She had truly been blessed. A man who looked good and was not full of himself was a hard one to find.

As she sat in the middle of the hall, she began to cry. Not an earth shattering cry that rocks your whole body, but slow and silent. It felt like letting go. Like that last bit of grief that had taken her eight years to get passed.

She began to wonder, *what if he comes back and sees David in his place? Would I even care?*

David had made no mention of wanting more than a friendship from her, but she could feel it radiating off him when they were together. His soft, searching, sad eyes no longer made her thing of Ryan but of the man who held them. There was a level of guilt that came with each tender moment between her and David that she felt like she was betraying Ryan in some way.

She touched his face in the picture, "Why can't I get away from you? You haunt me and I don't even know where you are. I really need to let you go."

At that moment she heard foot steps behind her. She turned to find David standing there, watching her, with those sad eyes.

"Are you alright, Emma? Do you need help?" he softly asked. He gave no indication that he had heard her words.

"Depends. Do you have a sleeping pill in your coat to help me sleep today away?" She could hear the sarcastic tone through the little laugh she gave him.

"Well, no, but I can sweep that up for you." She could see his concern for her and it endeared him to her even more.

She got up off the floor walked to him, hesitantly placed her hand on his arm, gave him her brave face, and said, "I am alright, David. It has been a tough morning. Truly, I will be okay."

"Well, if you are alright, then let me help you clean up this glass so you can do what you need to for dinner. I wasn't hungry until I stepped foot in your kitchen and smelled that turkey. It smells good." His smile stretched from ear to ear. It made her smile to see that smile. In fact, it warmed her heart. She reached for his hand and gave it a light squeeze.

"The broom is in the hall closet. Just be careful."

He squeezed her hand back in understanding and then let go as he went to the closet.

Things were about to change for them, she could feel it.

***

He had walked into Emma's house after knocking and waiting a couple of minutes. He called out to her, but there was no answer. It seemed like that happened a lot. The further he walked into the house, the louder her faint sniffles became. He followed the sound to the hall and stopped dead in his tracks when he heard her talk.

He hated that she felt like she couldn't move forward in her life. He hated the fact that she had been waiting all these years for him to come back.

God, make this end today. Give me a chance to tell her. Let this be the last day of her misery. I know I have been a fool, but this fool has seen the light. Show me what to do.

He swept up the broken glass of their wedding photo and he saw the relevance it had on their lives.

The glass was their lives. At first it was whole and beautiful, like the picture and frame. But life and poor choices broke that beautiful thing they had. Now he was going to have to 'man up' and sweep up the broken pieces and make it right again. And he knew he would be able to do it only with God's help.

***

They were all seated around the dinner table. A mound of beautifully cooked turkey sat before David. He had offered to carve it for her. Mashed potatoes with butter melting down the side, candied yams covered with marshmallows, green beans and carrots, cranberry relish sat with pickles and olives filled the table. She had the pies she made the night before warming in the oven. Looking at the table, you would think that she was feeding a small army. But she had a plan for it all, leftover meals for a week. Well maybe not quite a week since the boys are going through a growth spurt.

She had felt the frown and tension melt when she turned to see David standing there. He brought her comfort that she had not felt in a long time.

She watched him at the end of the table, carving that seventeen-pound turkey, laughing at a joke Aaron had just told him. All three kids looked happy too. They seemed whole again.

***

Stephen watched David carve the turkey and realized that it was nice to have a man around the house. He and David had had a couple of talks in the last few weeks. Guy stuff. He hadn't told his mom yet, but he figured since they had been going out for those walks on Sundays, that she wouldn't care.

He looked at her and saw she was watching David and noticed she had a strange smile on her face. One he had never seen before. He thought she looked beautiful. She looked light and calm as she watched him.

Stephen didn't understand all that was going on between them, but if it led to David becoming a permanent resident around the house, he was good with that.

He reached over to his mom, who sat next to him, and took her hand. "I'm sorry about earlier, Mom."

"It's okay Stephen, I forgive you."

Chapter 20

David still was a puzzle to her, but she didn't really care anymore. She wanted to know about him. There was still a nagging voice in the back of her mind that asked, *who was he?* What she did know about him was appealing to any woman but so many could not look past the scars and the limp. This man sitting across from her was nice, caring, thoughtful, and she could now add, fun. She had a good time whenever he was around.

She looked around at those who were sitting at the table. Kids all had smiles. Everyone seemed to be just as happy and content with him here as she was. David and the boys were having a conversation about football when she heard him ask them if they liked to play.

He looked up at her, "You mind if I take them outside to throw the ball around?"

"Um, sure! Yeah, that would be great. It'll give me time to clean up. It looks like someone might be going down for a little nap." She nodded her head in Sarah's direction and David caught her meaning. Sarah was half asleep at the table. Her sweet little head kept bobbing up and down as she dozed. Her elbow was on the table with her fork in the air. At the end of the fork was a rather large piece of turkey. They looked at each other and laughed quietly.

"She seems far enough along that she might need help getting upstairs. You want me to take her up?" he asked.

Her brain said "NO!" But her heart said, "You can trust him". She wanted to trust him. "Are you sure you can with your leg?"

"I'm having a good day today. I'll just have to take it slow."

"Well, if you're sure, I'll show you up. Boys, scrape the plates and I will do the rest. And finish your milk Aaron." She ordered. "David, go ahead and grab her and follow me up. It is a good thing you are here. I would have to leave her here at the table. She has gotten too big for me to carry." He seemed to happily comply.

He followed her up the stairs and into Sarah's room. He laid her down while Emma covered her up. She looked up at David and caught him watching Sarah sleep. She could see the longing in his eyes.

"Does this make you miss your family?"

"Yeah. I am realizing I am missing out on a lot." He shifted his gazed to Emma and said, "I hope God will give me a second chance, some day." He took a deep breath, looked back at Sarah, "Well, I guess it is time for some football." He looked again at Emma, "I promise to take it easy on them."

With a smirk and a small laugh, he left the room. Emma waited until she knew he was downstairs and outside with the boys. She had to talk to someone. She knew it was a holiday, but she needed clarity.

Normally she would call Ann, but she had a feeling this time she needed to call Pastor Cross. She wanted to leave him alone with his family, but she would try to be quick.

She walked down stairs and went for her phone that was on the counter and looked up the pastor's phone number and hesitantly pushed 'send'. She walked the floor as the phone rang on the other end. She didn't know what her questions were, but she knew she had them.

"Hello."

"Pastor Cross? This is Emma."

"Emma! Happy Thanksgiving! What can I do for ya? How has your afternoon been?"

"It's been…interesting to say the least. I have some questions for you. I'll try to make it quick though."

"Alright, let's hear it."

She paused a moment, not sure how to ask. "Are you still there, Emma?"

"What? Yes, just trying to get the wording right."

"Oh this is a big deal. Let me turn off the TV here so I can focus."

That broke her tension a bit and it made her giggle. There was no background noise on his end to indicate he was watching the television.

"Okay, ready when you are dear."

"I know you meet with David on Mondays..."

"Did he tell you that?"

"Yes"

"Then I will confirm it."

"Is he…" She looked out the kitchen window to see him toss the ball. "Is he trustworthy?"

"Yes, I would say so. He has given me no reason not to trust him."

"Good, because I invited him over for supper today."

"Wow! Well that was nice of you. Seems like a big step for you."

"We have actually been having Sunday dinner together for the last three weeks. When I found out he would be alone today, I invited him over."

"I see."

"Pastor, something is happening, but I need to know first."

"Just ask me whatever it is you want to know. Keep in mind though, I may not be able to answer your question."

"I can accept that." She paused for a minute, trying to get a hold of everything going through her head. "Oh, I'll just come right out and ask - Is he Ryan?" She let out the breath she was holding because she felt dizzy, but when there was no answer right away, she found herself holding it again. It made her pulse race and her head spin. The anticipation of his answer made her crazy.

"Emma, did he tell you he was?"

"Well, no, but the things he has been saying and the way he acts, even the way we work together in the kitchen seems so natural, like Ryan and I did. I just need to know."

"If he is Ryan, how would you feel about it?"

"I'm not sure. I have been running this through my brain the last three weeks."

"And if he isn't, will it change anything?"

Emma thought for a minute. "I guess, not really."

"So does it really matter?"

"I guess not."

"Hmmm, interesting," was his quiet reply. "Alright, let me just say this then. If he is Ryan, let him reveal himself when he is ready. I can imagine that he deals with enough guilt for leaving you. If he isn't Ryan, then enjoy the friendship you are building. Just follow his lead, okay?"

"Pastor Cross? You know the answer, don't you?"

"Yes, dear, I do. But it is not for me to tell you. Trust, hon. You need to trust him, me and most importantly, God. When it is time, you'll know. What is your gut telling you?"

"That he is Ryan."

"Very interesting. Trust, Emma. God would not lead you down this path if it was bad for you and the kids. You believe that?"

"Yes."

"Okay then, just enjoy your time getting to know the man and don't worry so much about it. The man won't hurt you or the kids. Alright?"

"Yes. Thank you Pastor. Have a good evening."

"You too."

She felt a bit more at peace as she hung up the call. "Just go with it Emma. It has been long enough" she told herself.

Now feeling like she was on more solid ground, she put her phone down and went to the sink to wash the dishes. When she glanced outside, she found herself having to do a double take. There in her backyard, in forty-degree weather, were three bare chests. All three males had stripped themselves of their shirts. The boys were no surprise to her. They walk around the house bare chested all the time, but David, well, he surprised her.

She knew that staring at the man was probably not a good thing. Her heart rate increased, blood surged through her veins and she felt her face flush. His years of being a "Jack of all trades" as he had put it, had been good to him. But the longer she looked at him, the more his scars became obvious. Half of his torso was covered in burns. She could now follow the line of burns from head to toe, well she guessed to his toes.

The excitement of seeing such a well-built man in her backyard shifted to compassion. He had clearly been through something traumatic.

She could see why he would think everyone thought him a monster. It reminded her of the comic strip pictures she had seen in Aaron's room of Batman and one of the villains, Two Face. She knew David wasn't evil, just the scars made him look that way.

Her hands flew to her face, because she could feel the sorrow for this man build up in her chest. She could easily imagine the horrific tragedy that this man endured because it was probably much like Ryan's. Her hands were soapy but she didn't notice. She couldn't control her cries. She was glad she was inside and they were out there. But then, David turned sideways, giving her full view of his left profile. It was not burned and scarred only a little, and her heart stopped and she gasped. *Just like Ryan.*

"Oh God, it is him!" She whispered. She was having a hard time breathing, but she knew without a doubt now. She studied that profile often enough to be burned into her brain, and her heart. It was unmistakable now. "Why didn't I see it before?"

"Mama, are you okay?" Sarah had awakened from her nap.

"Yeah Honey." She wiped the tears from her face with her hands, trying to hide the emotion. She didn't want to scare her little girl. "Why don't you go start a movie? I will go get your brothers. Mr. David and I need to talk."

"Can we have popcorn?"

"Yeah, I'll have Stephen get it going. Go on now."

Emma grabbed her coat of the coat rack, walked out the back door to the porch and called the boys.

"Stephen! Aaron! Inside! Now Please!" *Mama has to have a talk with your Dad!*

***

The tone of her voice caused all three of them to stop what they were doing. The boys looked at each other and then at him with understanding that someone was in trouble. It most likely would be him.

"Go on, she sounds upset."

That was an understatement. He knew what that tone of voice meant. He heard it plenty of times when the boys were little. At least she didn't use their middle names. If he really thought about it, she had scolded him a time or two with that tone when they were first married.

Seeing her this way reminded him why he had tried so hard push this image from his mind. She was beautiful and sweet most of the time, with her golden hair and bright blue eyes, but when she got irritated with him, she made him think of some Nordic warrior princess. Oh yeah, that got him in even more trouble one time.

They had been standing in the kitchen, and she was giving him her "what for" about him leaving laundry on the living room floor, and all he could do was look her up and down and grin stupidly at how stunning she looked at that moment. That had made her even madder because she thought he wasn't listening now. He wasn't. She was yelling at him with all the fire and spirit that he knew she had possessed, and all he wanted to do was pick her up, cradle her in his arms, and carry her down the hall. When her hand came up to smack him for not listening, he grabbed that hand, pulled her to him, and did just what he was thinking about. The roast was burned that day but neither of them worried about it. They had enjoyed the whole evening locked in their room, only coming out for the necessities – crackers, peanut butter and water - and back to the bedroom. He had a suspicion Stephen was a result of that evening but he would never tell. That was a moment meant for them alone.

Now, all these years later, his feisty princess was standing in front of him again. The only problem was this time, he had no rights to her. She was not his anymore. They were not married. He had to keep his cool now. No sweeping her off her feet tonight, or any night for that matter. For now.

He watched the boys make their way to the house and gave a meek wave in response to theirs. "Sleep good, guys!"

"You too, Mr. David. It was nice knowing you!" Aaron said. That got a scowl out of her as he passed her on the deck. He had to smile at the image.

"Don't you worry about me. I can handle it."

He then heard Aaron say, "Don't count on it."

If they only knew.

He then heard her give instructions to make popcorn and watch a movie with Sarah. As he watched his boys go into the house, he felt pride swell again within his chest. They are good boys. Emma then turned her sights back on him. A wealth of emotions crossed her face but there were three he knew well - anger, sadness and confusion.

Chapter 21

She was not sure what to feel now that she was alone with him. It wasn't like before. Before, there was just suspicion of who he was. A friendship had built between them. Now she knew, without a shadow of a doubt. He was her Ryan. The man who made her stomach do cartwheels every time he walked into the room. The man who had treated her with such tenderness and care no matter how wicked she would be toward him. The man who made her knees weak with every single kiss, including the light peck her gave her on the cheek the last time she saw him before the accident.

She remembered that day with such disgust. Not in him, but in herself. She had been mean to him and merciless when he apologized. That afternoon had haunted her every night. She could have been nicer. She could have shown forgiveness. Instead she ignored him and let him leave doubting how much she really needed him.

No wonder he had decided she could do better without him. Not once had she indicated she needed him since Stephen was born. She had somehow, during that first pregnancy, learned to do things without him. It took divorce papers for her to see it though. Now, eight years later, here he was, standing in her backyard. In the freezing cold, snow starting to fall, still missing his shirt, which made her a bit nervous and heart sick.

His torso was mix of muscles and scars. Seeing all of the pain in those marks left on his body from the fire broke her heart.

"Please put your shirt on, I can't think." She heard the frustration in her voice as she said it. "I'm sorry, that was harsh. Just give me a minute." She closed her eyes, bowed her head, took a deep breath and said a quick prayer. *Lord, you have brought him back to us. I can't face these emotions on my own. I can't face him and say all I need to without your help. Help me to say what I need to and show him kindness.*

She lifted her head to see that he had moved toward her and was now standing five feet from her. At that moment, her heart began to race, and she could feel the pressure build on the back side of her eyes. Her muscles tightened up and she tried to relax, as she squeezed her hands a few times. It didn't work. She couldn't talk or move. All she could do was look at him. She didn't know which emotion to feel first.

***

He saw her struggle. In the way she moved her hands but stood stone still. He could see her chest rise and fall in shallow breaths. He could see the tears pooling in her eyes. She was even having a hard time talking. He could see the gears rolling, but her mouth wouldn't let her speak it. So, he would force her.

"Say it, Emma. Just say it." She shook her head in response.

He took another step toward her. He could see her breathing get even faster. If she didn't say what he knew in his heart she wanted to, she was going to pass out from the lack of oxygen.

"Say it before you pass out, honey." That got her attention.

In a soft whisper she said, "I can't", while she was still shaking her head in disbelief.

***

Emma knew she had to say something, but she didn't know where to start. She had been dreaming for years that this would happen and now that it had. Nothing was coming out of her mouth. She was stunned.

She felt a tear run down her cheek and before she could reach up to wipe it away, his thumb brushed at her cheek, and her breathing stopped.

"Emma, honey, I can see that you know the truth now. I knew I couldn't hide from you for long, but you have to say something."

A breathy "Ryan?" was all she could say. She had to think carefully what came out next.

"Yes," was his only response. It sounded like music when she said his name and not called him David. Sweet, beautiful music.

He was taken aback by what she did next but he knew he had to let her. He deserved it.

The tears poured from her eyes, like someone had turned on the faucet in a sink, and with a shrill-like sound, she started pounding on him. They weren't lightweight, soft as a feather pounding either. Quite a few of the hits had hurt. He knew though that this physical pain was small compared to what he put her through.

She was getting stronger with each hit to his chest. He reached out to grab her shoulders to brace himself so he didn't to fall over on her.

She hadn't noticed. He had a need to touch her, even if she was pelting him with her fists. He then felt his breath catch and felt the tears in his own eyes build pressure. That's when she looked up at him, stopped hitting his chest, let out a couple of heart wrenching sobs and went limp. The weight of her falling in his arms caused him to lose balance and the both fell in a heap to the ground.

They knelt in the yard, holding each other like it was their last day on earth. She didn't pull away from him; he wasn't sure he would let her if she tried. He didn't think he would ever let her go again. No matter what happened after tonight, he would never leave her side again. He would do his best to be the man she needed and the kind of dad his kids needed. Even if she only let him be a father to their children and not her husband. His running was over.

He whispered in her ear, "I'm not running anymore."

***

Stephen had expected to hear mom yelling at David by now. He figured they needed some private time and had to talk about grown up things.   Aaron and Sarah were in the living room watching a movie and he was getting a drink when he thought he heard the agonizing mew of a cat. So he looked out the window to try to see, but it was dark and he couldn't see anything close to the house.

Just as he turned from the window to go back to the movie, something caught his attention out in the yard. When he turned back and focused more on what was out there, all he could see was a large mound out in the yard. With the moonlight shining down on what he was looking at, he thought it looked like mom and David huddled on the ground. He was now confused and called his brother and sister to the back door to look too. They confirmed that they were seeing the same thing as him.

"Do I go out?" He asked them. They both just shrugged their shoulders. Something was happening, but they didn't know what to do about it, so they just stood there, watching, hoping everything was okay.

Chapter 22

They were not sure how long they had held each other, but neither of them seemed to want to let go of the other. They seemed to have held on for dear life. They knew the air around them was cool but inside their huddle, it was as warm as the summer sun. All the years of heartache and tears. The years of drinking away the pain. All the anger and bitterness that had built up between them fell away with the tears that filled their eyes. The embrace they shared seemed to crush the concrete walls they had built up around their hearts. It was healing.

What now? Emma thought as they slowly began to stand up.

She could tell he was not ready to let her go, but she had to think and she couldn't when wrapped in his arms. She helped him as he tried to stand. Now the nerves and uncertainty returned. She wasn't sure what to do next.

"What's going through your mind, Emma? I can see the gears turning behind those beautiful, baby blues." His lazy grin did strange things to her insides. She found she loved and hated it all at the same time. She felt the need to protect herself until she knew what was next.

"Don't pretend you still know me, David, er Ryan. Whichever name you go by now. Don't act like nothing is changed! Everything is different now. I am different. You're different. And don't even get me started on the kids."

She put her hand to her chest to try to calm her racing heart. She began to shift her weight from one leg to the other. She needed to think and she couldn't.

"You're right. We have all changed. But what I realize, right now, in this moment, is I love you. I am not sure I ever stopped. I am not walking away again. I am a different man, but a better man. A stronger man. A man who wants and needs to take responsibility for his family." He looked down at their feet, placed his hands in his pocket. She could see the nervous school boy she once knew. "Well, that is if he has a family to take responsibility for. Do I still have that family, Emma? Can we work things out?"

She didn't know what to think or say. A war raged within her. One side wanted to yell *'yes'* so loud that the whole world could hear it and then leap into his arms. Then there was the other side. This side was the side that kept her heart safe from the hurt and pain; the part that had to think of ways to survive in this world. It had been her and the kids for so long that she wasn't sure how to bring him back into the mix.

"I don't know. I, I mean we, we have to think of the kids. What will they think? I have a feeling Stephen suspects. I have to put them first."

Ryan stepped forward and grabbed her arms, almost in desperation. She could see it in his blazing eyes. "But what about you, Emma? What do you want? If you don't want me, then I won't try anymore to win your heart, but what do you want?"

"I don't know!" She pushed back, it was safe to push him away. She felt safe in his hands, but the survivor told her to push away. "I don't know what I want. I am so confused. Maybe you just need to go home for tonight and we can talk about it later. I need time, Ryan. Do you understand that? I need time."

At that moment, Stephen poked his head out the back door, "Ma? You okay?"

"Yeah Baby! Say goodnight to Mr. David and then head for bed."

"Good Night, Mr. David!"

"Good Night Buddy!"

She could hear the catch in his voice as he said it. She knew she was breaking his heart right now, but she had to think. He looked back to her. He reached out with his hand, and lightly cupped his hand on her cheek and slowly stroked it with his thumb. Then in a whisper, he said, "Good Night, sweet Emma."

She felt the shock of electricity shoot through her like a lightning bolt, and then it seemed to ignite a fire that started in her heart and flowed through her veins. She felt her head instinctively turn into his hand for just a split second, and then she came back to her senses, and righted herself.

"Good Night, Ryan." She tried to give him a blank stare, but with that cocky grin on his face, she could tell he was not fooled.

"You don't have to hide from me." He turned and walked toward the back of her property, toward the pond. Confused even more, she walked after him.

"Where are you going?"

"Home. Didn't you notice I didn't drive here? My property backs up to yours. We're neighbors. Have been all along. So anytime you need a cup of sugar, well, you know where I am." She stopped in her tracks as she watched the trees fold in around him.

He disappeared into the darkness.

"Don't you need a flashlight?" she yelled to him.

Faintly she heard him respond, "I know my way, Honey! Don't worry yourself." She could hear the smile in his voice.

She turned back toward the house and yard, and surveyed everything, trying to process the night's events.

What is so wrong in letting him back in?

"Because I don't know if my heart can handle it again."

Why don't you just trust that I know what I am doing? You were not meant to do this alone.

"But I have. We've done alright, haven't we? God I am not sure I can do it. I want to, but I don't if I can trust him, or my heart. It is still hard to forgive him. I'm just not sure if I'm there yet."

Why do you think I brought you back here?

"For the kids?"

You don't sound too sure of yourself. Just trust Me. I know the plans I have for you and your family. Plans to prosper you and bring you...

"Hope. Okay! But I am still scared, God. I am scared to death."

Once she said *'okay'* to God, the exhaustion folded in on her and she felt weak and tired. So she slowly made her way to the house, closed things up for the night, and went to bed. Tomorrow was a new day, and maybe she would be able to think better after a good night's rest.

***

He stood in the tree line, yet again. He wasn't ready to leave, but he understood that she needed space. He heard her talking to herself, he assumed she was praying, or giving God an earful. She seemed to do that quite a bit. He could hear the war raging in her mind. *I'll give her time, even though it might kill me.*

Typically, the moon made a wonderful guide, but when he came to the thick parts of the wooded overgrowth, he really had to grope around in the dark to find his way. He knew these woods well, but was having a hard time finding his way through. The moon was nowhere to be seen in the thicket. The wind blew hard and he was concerned that it would knock him over a few times.

He heard a twig snap behind him and the hair on his neck stood on end. He turned to see if someone was there.

"Hello!"

Nothing. No one was there. There was a looming sense of danger lurking in the air the closer he got to his house. In this part of the state there weren't many wild predators, but there were rumors that a cougar had been seen and quite a few coyotes. David knew that if these two breeds of animals were hungry enough, they would attack.

He began to walk again for home, but was now more alert of his surroundings.

"Lord, watch over me and show me how to get home safely."

The eeriness never left him the entire walk home but he was glad to see his back porch light.

As he approached the house, he heard a sound that resembled something heavy falling and then breaking. It was coming from within the house. He quietly walked up the back steps of the house to look in the kitchen window. Through that window he could see straight to the front door. He could see that his freezer door was hanging open as well as all his kitchen cupboards. The few dishes he had, were now broken on the counter tops and floors. Some of the drawers were laying awkwardly on the floor.

He looked in the direction of his living room. There was the silhouette of a tall, well-built man standing near his television. Quickly sizing him up, David figured he was a little bigger than himself. He felt every muscle in his body began to twitch and tighten as he noticed another man stride into view. He could feel the joy of what happened between him and Emma fall away and the space was now filled with anger and aggression.

"I have so little to begin with and these punks have broken most of it. This has to stop! Now!" He knew that if Emma was with him, she would tell him to think of the kids. He reasoned that he was being a good example by protecting what is yours. He slowly reached for the back door and quietly opened it.

He stood in the stairway to his basement that was just inside the door, and listened. He could hear hushed, angry whispers. Comments about "not much here worth taking" and "this was a waste of time". David figured after that they would have left, but he could tell they were still digging around and trashing his place more. He knew they wouldn't find anything, so he got a little cocky and stepped into the kitchen.

He stood in the middle of the kitchen, leaned lazily on his cane and watched the guys toss his living room. He had had enough.

"You about done tossing my home? You boys won't find anything here, so how about you get out of here."

The men turned on him. That's when he caught the glint of something metallic in the one guy's hand. The moonlight coming through the front window gave the gun a shining gleam. It was now pointed right at him.

He knew the table had just turned.

"What are you going to do about it? What if we just want to toss a place?" said the guy with the gun.

"Just shoot him and let's go. He's seen us now. He's crippled, not like he'll chase us." said the other guy.

He watched them and the gun as they chose that moment to argue about whether or not to shoot him. He stood there, clutching his fist trying to keep calm. His automatic response to protect himself kicked in, but the rational part of him kept saying, *"Stay still, you just found your family. Don't blow it."*

He tried to just stay there and wait for them to leave. Unfortunately, he remembered something his granddad told him, *"A man doesn't let strangers disrespect him on his own property."* He started to walk toward the guys.

He must have startled them again because as he heard a loud bang ring through the air, felt something hit him in the right side of his chest. Then he watched them run out the front of the house.

In his mind, it was like watching a movie in slow motion.

He didn't even realize he had made enough of an advance on them to startle them. He didn't even see the guy raise the gun again, but judging from the burning pain radiating through his body, he knew what happened.

He couldn't move. He was shocked. He couldn't move his right arm and he was finding it hard to breathe. He patted his pocket for the phone. The stress on the body to just pull the phone out of his pocket was enough to bring him to his knees. He didn't just kneel, he crashed to his knees. The pain of the fall shot right up into his hips and spine.

He finished lowering himself to the floor as carefully as possible. He had just enough time to dial 911 before the pain became too much and he began to fade out. He could hear the dispatch lady on the other end, but couldn't respond. His last thought before his world going completely dark was, *God, not again.*

Chapter 23

Emma thought for sure Ryan would be back the next day or at least on Saturday, but she did not see or hear from him since Thanksgiving night. It worried her a bit, but she was also glad of it. She needed a few days to think and pray. She felt like a mess. The kids were asking her constantly if she was okay. She hated that they didn't know but she was not going to say anything without Ryan there to tell them himself.

Come Sunday morning, she was content in letting him into their lives enough so the kids would know him. As far as working things out between them, well that was going to take more time. She was already beginning to feel the seeds of love bloom again, but that was before, when she thought he was just David.

She was in the middle of blowing her hair dry when Stephen came to the bathroom door with her cell phone in his hand. She was startled when he touched her shoulder.

"What d'ya need?" she yelled over the noise.

"Mom, Pastor Cross is on the phone." He handed her the device.

She took the phone as she put the hair dryer down. "Hello Pastor! What can I do for you?" This was a strange thing for him to call her on a Sunday, but she figured it couldn't wait a half an hour if he was calling.

"I need you to get here sooner than normal.

I need to talk with you and the kids before service." All her internal alarms began to go off.

"Pastor, what's wrong?"

"Just get here as soon as possible. Go through the back of the church and to my office. Don't come through the front." She thought his request was strange but would comply. The man never gave instructions like that without a reason.

"Okay Pastor. I'll be there in fifteen minutes. I was about done getting ready anyhow."

They hung up and she told the kids to make sure they were ready and to get out to the vehicle. "The bus leaves in ten minutes!" She yelled from the top of the stairs. Aaron gave a smart mouth comment about not owning a bus. "Now is not the time son, do as you are told. Pastor wants to talk to us before service so we need to get there before we normally do."

They were all out of the drive within ten minutes and on their way to the church. She could feel the panic rising up in her chest. The hair on her neck and arms was standing on end and she was feeling edgy. Thankfully the kids could sense something was wrong as well. No one said a word all the way to the church.

She parked on the back side of the church and they ran in the back door. "Head for his office, do not stop to say 'Hi' to anyone."

They walked in the office to see Pastor Cross and his wife. They were praying so they walked in quietly.

Pastor looked up and told Stephen to shut the door. Emma was frightened now.

Something about this felt familiar. She sensed something bad had happened, but she couldn't figure out who it might be that he would want to pull her aside like this. She hadn't called him back after she discovered that David was really Ryan. Maybe something happened to her dad or mom?

"Pastor, you're scaring me, what is this about?" She looked at each of the kids, and saw Stephen was thinking the same thing.

"Oh, Emma." Mrs. Cross came and sat next to her and held her hand. She looked back at Pastor.

"Emma, were your questions answered Thursday night that you had called me about?"

"Yes. They were."

"Were your suspicions correct?"

"Yes. Where is this going?"

"Do the kids know yet?"

She hesitantly shook her head 'no'. She seemed to lose her ability to talk when she was catching on that something really had happened to Ryan. *God, please don't tell me he is gone for good now.* She began to fear the worst.

"Had you decided to tell them?"

"Yes, but I hadn't talked to him yet about it."

"Alright, you need to tell them, now! Right here. Something has happened and word has spread like a wildfire. Honestly, I am surprised you don't know what happened yet."

"I haven't heard anything from him since Thursday night. I thought for sure he would have at least called. Pastor, what happened? Please tell me."

"He went into his home and startled some men who were in the process of robbing him." Emma began to shake her head. She felt the dam of tears building up on the back of her eyes burst open. Pastor Cross leaned forward and took her hands in his. "Emma, he is alive, but he was shot. His identity was released in the paper this morning. I was called because I was his emergency contact and I had to reveal his real name. He woke enough to nod that I was telling the truth."

He paused enough to let the information process. "So I need to tell the kids now, before they go out there for service. Is that what you are saying?" She could feel the room begin to tilt and spin.

"Yes. Or you can just head home, or to the hospital. But these kids need to know, because all their friends know now."

"Mama?" Sarah's sweet, questioning voice broke through all that was going through her mind.

"Okay. Um..." She looked to the pastor and his wife for some kind of comfort. "How do I say this?"

"Just let it out sweetie" Mrs. Cross told her.

"You want us to leave?"

"No. I need support. I feel like I could pass out right now." She turned back to the kids. She watched them for a moment while she tried to think of a way to break the news to them. Stephen broke the silence.

"Mom? Is it Mr. David?" That's one way to start. The kid was so intuitive.

"Yes, it is Mr. David. But Mr. David is not who we thought he was. Mommy didn't realize it until Thursday night. I wanted him to tell you himself, but it looks like he can't right now." She paused and took a deep breath. She had admitted it in her mind and to Ryan, but not out loud for everyone to hear. "Mr. David is...well...really, he is your daddy."

Sarah began to cry. Stephen looked like a deer caught in the headlights. Aaron darted from the room and then she heard him start to sob out in the hall. She got up to get him and brought him back in.

***

I knew it! God, I knew it. I could feel it. I don't know why, but I could feel it. It really is him.

Stephen felt stunned but was glad of this news. He didn't know why his dad did what he did, but he was just so happy to have the man back in his life that he didn't care. He thought it was cool that the man who had been spending time with them was not just a friend, but his dad.

His mom's voice broke his trance.

"Like I said, I didn't realize it until Thursday night. I wanted us to be together to tell you kids. Not like this."

"Why didn't you say something then, Mom?" Aaron yelled at her from the hall.

"I was in shock myself honey. I couldn't even think."

Sarah went to their mom. "Can we go see d-d-daddy?" Stephen could see the tears begin to fall down his sister's face.

He took this moment to agree. "Mom, let's go see dad."

He watched as his mom left the room to talk to Aaron, "Would you like to go see him too?" Aaron must have just nodded his head yes.

"Alright then, let's go see your daddy." She came back in the room, "I guess we will not be in service this morning."

"That's fine. If you were, I would have been a little concerned. Can I say something in the service?"

"Did, David, I mean Ryan say to?" It sounded as weird to Stephen as it must have been to his mom to say. "We aren't married anymore so I can't speak for him."

"He did give his blessing for his part. Do I have your blessing on your part?"

"I suppose, not much to say besides we just found out ourselves."

"Do you trust me to do the right thing, Emma?"

"Yes." She stood up, hugged Pastor and Mrs. Cross and then looked at him and his brother and sister. "Let's go kids."

Stephen was more than ready. He had thought on Thursday that it would be wonderful if Mr. David could be a part of their lives permanently but the fact that he was his real dad was even better.

He walked to his mom and took her hand and said, "Let's go Mom."

Chapter 24

There she was, standing right in front of him, dressed in a white dress that flowed with the breeze. Her beautiful face smiled at him and it warmed him through to the bone and made the ache disappear. Her eyes sparkled in the light like sapphires. Her hair hung loose around her shoulders and down her back. Her golden hair had the glow of a halo and it made her look like an angel. He wanted to reach out and run his fingers through it like he once had. He took a step toward her, but the distance hadn't changed between them. So he took another step, but still, she was just as far from him as she once was. He continued to walk toward her, feeling more and more confused with each useless step. As he felt panic creep up, he began to run for her, but still, the distance had not changed. He could see her, her arms were stretched out to him. He could faintly hear the sound of her voice crying out to him to "Just reach out". Every time he did, their fingertips would barely touch and then the space between them grew again. He didn't know what to do anymore. In frustration, he ran his hand over his face and through his hair and realized his face was streaked with tears and his hair was damp with sweat from running to her. He didn't realize he had been crying, but he knew why. The woman he loved more than his own life was just out of his reach. As he started running for her again, he felt a hand on his head. He stopped dead in his tracks and looked around in confusion. He looked up and saw nothing, but he felt it. Like someone petting his head. He tried to shake it off, but then when he looked back at Emma, she was gone and he looked into blackness. Then he heard her voice. "Ryan, wake up. Please. We need you to wake up."

His eyes flew open and before him was his beautiful Emma with her eyes glistening like water in the sun light. "What happened? Where am I?"

"Ryan, you're in the hospital, remember?"

"The burglary. Man that was stupid." He was embarrassed to admit he acted before he thought.

"How are you feeling?" She was holding his hand and gently rubbing his hand with her thumb.

He found the action very soothing.

"What are you doing here? Who told you I was here?"

"Pastor Cross called us in this morning to tell us what happened. We decid..."

"Wait, we? Who else is here?" He picked his head up to look around the room and saw no one.

"The kids, Ryan. They're in the hall. They're waiting, well, waiting to see their dad."

"What?!" He sat up without thinking and felt a shooting pain pierce him in his side. He looked down at his right side, remembering he couldn't move so quick.

He looked back at Emma. "Did you tell the kids? Alone?"

"I had to. Your name was released in the papers this morning and everyone in church knows. Pastor wanted to be sure we knew before the kids got word through the gossip mill. You ready to see them?"

"How did they react? I mean, are they okay?"

"They are fine. In fact they chose to come here instead of sit through service. We are here on their request." He didn't like how that sounded.

"You mean you wouldn't be here if they didn't want to?"

"Ryan, let's not do that now. Let's just let the kids come in and see you. Sarah is eager to 'meet' her daddy. She is beside herself."

He nodded his head and Emma left the room to go get the kids. They were all hesitant to come through the door without Emma leading the way. He thought it interesting to watch. He just played football with the boys a couple of days ago but right now, they were looking at him like he was a stranger.

"It's alright guys, come on in. I'm okay."

Stephen came right to the side of the bed, leaned over and hugged Ryan's neck. "I knew it was you, Dad. I don't know how, but I knew. I knew it." He kept repeating himself and didn't let go. Ryan had to push him back a bit. He was squeezing his neck so hard, Ryan was having a hard time breathing.

"Boy, you are getting strong. You're killing me here. Loosen up a bit," he said with a laugh and both of them looked at each other with big grins on their faces.

"I am glad you figured it out." He pulled his oldest son a little closer to him and whispered in his ear, "took your mom long enough." They both started to laugh at that.

"Okay let me hug the other two."

Stephen stepped back and went to his mom and wrapped his arms around her like he did as a toddler. It warmed his heart.

Next Sarah came to his bedside. He could see her bottom lip quiver and tears begin to pool in the corners of her eyes. "Is it really you?"

"Yes baby girl, I am so sorry I left you. Do you forgive me?"

She stood there for a moment and then nodded her head.

"Good, can I have a hug now? I haven't held you since you were three weeks old."

Sarah leaped on to the bed and wrapped her arms around him. The movement of the bed made his side hurt again, but he didn't care. He was holding his baby girl again. It was worth the physical pain. After a minute or two, she nestled in on his left side and with her head on his shoulder, she began to pat the right side of his face. The action broke his heart. He looked up at that moment and saw Aaron standing at the end of his bed. He looked like he was ready to lash out. *Just like his mama.*

"Sarah, why don't you go to your mama, I think Aaron has something to say." Sarah got down off the bed and went to her mom and crawled in her lap. Emma was seated in the chair in the corner of the room. Quiet as ever.

"Come here Bud, and let me have it. But don't hit me like your mom did, not until I have healed a bit." Aaron went to Ryan's side and was looking down at him. "Say what's on your mind, Aaron."

"I am mad at you." He was honest.

"Okay. I can understand that. Want to tell me why?"

"You left."

"I was a fool."

"Yes, you were." *Just like his mom.*

"Anything else you want to say or do?"

"I want to…to...I don't know."

"Can you sit right here?" Ryan patted the bed. Aaron sat down, hesitantly. "Can I ask you something?" Aaron nodded his head. "Can you forgive me? I was dumb and I thought I was doing something good for you guys. I thought you would all be better off without me. I realized over the last couple of months that was not the case. I am sorry."

Aaron sat and watched Ryan for a moment. Then leaned over and did as his brother and sister had, and wrapped his arms around his neck and squeezed. He patted Aaron's back and said, "Little looser Bud, I can't breathe."

When Aaron relaxed a bit, Ryan held his second born a little longer than he had the others. He truly missed out on so much with Aaron, and even more with Sarah.

He caught movement from the corner of the room as Emma got up and walked to the bed. He could feel the tension radiating off of her. It felt like his dream. She was here in front of him, yet she was so far away. He felt closer to her as David than he did now as Ryan.

"Alright Aaron, we need to let your dad rest. We can come back after school tomorrow."

"They are releasing me tomorrow possibly. Can I call you and let you know?"

She let out a heavy sigh, "Alright, that's fine. Do you have a ride home if they do?"

"Yes, Pastor Cross is coming."

"Mommy? Is daddy coming to stay with us now?" Sarah looked up at her mom with hope in her eyes. Emma looked uneasy so he spoke for her.

"Sarah, honey, come here." She walked to him. "Mommy and Daddy are not married right now, so it wouldn't be right for me to stay at your house. Do you understand that?" She nodded her head.

"So will you get married now?" Sarah asked.

"That is something we have yet to talk about. There hasn't been a lot of time to talk." He looked up at Emma and caught her startled look. He looked at her pointedly, "But we will be talking about it, soon. Right, Emma?"

"Maybe but you have to worry about getting better, first."

He could tell she was putting him off, but it just encouraged him more. He wouldn't be letting go so easily this time.

The kids came and gave him a tight hug and walked out of the room. Emma stayed behind and looked at him.

She came to the bed, grabbed his hand and gave it a squeeze. "I am glad you are alright. I was worried."

"Were you really?" The idea of her being worried about him made him feel a little more confident in how things were going to play out.

"Yes, Ryan. I am not totally heartless." He knew that this act of being indifferent was just her trying to keep her wall in place and he was determined to bring it down. To drive that point home, he ran his thumb across the top of her hand. It had always been his signal to her that he still loved her.

"Emma, I am a patient man, but please don't put this off longer than necessary. We both know we need to talk about some things. In my defense, let me say, I am sorry. For all of it, the wasted time and neglecting you. I know how bitter you feel toward me. I cannot blame you, but I hope you can forgive me and we can fix this."

She slowly nodded and squeezed his hand and then walked out of the room.

Chapter 25

Emma woke earlier than usual every morning for the past week. Sleep seemed to avoid her almost every night. She dreamed of him often. Seeing him lying in that hospital bed again just put her back eight years. She was really unsure how she was going to function while teaching today. Coffee and prayer. That's what will get me through the day.

With her elbows on her desk, she put her head in her hands and began to talk to God. "How am I going to handle this, God? I want to scream at him and kiss him all at once."

"Well that's a start."

Emma picked her head up and saw her sister-in-law, Tiffany, at the back of the classroom standing in the doorway. Excitement filled Emma at seeing her and she felt a slight rejuvenation. "What are you doing here? Why didn't you call and tell me you were coming to town today? How long are you here for?" As Emma rattled off all her questions, she had walked to Tiffany to embrace her sister. The two women stood in the doorway, hugging one another. Finally, Tiffany stepped back a bit and watched her sister.

"I received a phone call yesterday, Emma. I figured you needed some family right now." Emma couldn't think for the life of her, who had called that would cause Tiffany to have this look of sympathy on her face.   "Ryan called me, Emma. He told me everything. Even though I already knew it was him. I am sorry I didn't tell you who David was sooner. I wanted to protect you both. I hope you don't hate me."

Emma was taken aback by this revelation. She took a step back and proceeded to pace the floor of her classroom, trying to process this information. She stopped and looked at her sister with total confusion on her face and in her voice, "You knew? How? When?"

Tiffany proceeded to tell her about Halloween night when Sarah had broken her arm.

Emma was in shock at the news. "He was there? At the hospital? Why didn't he say anything?" She didn't know how to handle all this new information. She didn't know how to handle anything that had happened in the last seven days. She felt like she didn't know which end was up and wanted to be with in the safety of her home. She began a frantic pace on the floor again. She was startled by her sister's hand on her arm.

"Emma, are you done for the day? Let's get you home."

The next hour was a haze to her. She wasn't sure how she had gotten home but she felt glad to be in a safe place. She halfheartedly climbed the stairs to her bedroom, and changed into something a little more comfortable. She could hear her sister-in-law on the phone while she took off her makeup and put her earrings away. She felt numb to everything now and was on autopilot. She just didn't know what to do. She felt lost and, like the flag on her front porch, waving in the cold breeze.

Emma walked to the window that overlooked the backyard. Her eyes fixed on the place in the yard that she finally confronted her missing husband. She just didn't know where to start in the process. "God? What now?"

"That's a good place to start, sis." Emma turned to see Tiffany standing behind her with a cup of chamomile tea handed out to her. "Talking to Him is always the best place to start."

"Tiff, where do I go from here? What would you do? Besides pray of course"

"Do you still love my brother?"

"I think so, but at the same time, I am so mad that having him around right now would be very bad for his health. Well worse than he is right now." She then remembered she was supposed to take the kids to see Ryan. Then Emma realized someone was missing. "Where are the kids?"

"Your friend Ann took them home with her. I told her you needed a break."

Emma hugged her sister, "Thank you Tiff. You are right. I need a break. Let's go downstairs and talk."

They made their way to the back of the house, Emma's thinking room.

The sisters sat there in silence. Emma turned on the electric fireplace. She didn't know if her being cold was the weather or the shock of the last week, but she couldn't get warm.

Emma looked into her cup, trying to think of a way to ask her next question, but finally decided straight forward was best, "Do you forgive him?"

"Yes."

"If your husband did this to you, would you take him back?"

"I can't answer that; it didn't happen to me."

"Okay, do your mom and dad know?"

"Yes we did a three-way call. He told us all at once. Even though he knew that I already knew."

"How do they feel about this?"

"Relieved. In fact, they are on their way here now. Mom has this need to take care of her injured boy." There was a pause as tension filled the air. "Emma, did you forgive him?"

"I thought I had, but now I find myself feeling happy and furious all at once. Thursday night, when I realized it was him in my backyard playing football with the boys, I was dumbfounded. And when I broke down and he caught me and held me, it was like I was whole again. Then reality hit me and I pushed him and that feeling away. When Pastor Cross told me about the robbery and shooting, I felt like a repeat of a bad movie from eight years ago. I just don't know where to go next."

"Sounds like you doubted yourself, him, and God. Ever think this is all orchestrated by God?"

"A little."

"Then let God finish guiding you. Emma, you know how to do this, why are you fighting it? Are you happy he is safe?"

"Well, yes."

"Then start there and let God do the rest."

At that moment, a truck pulled in the driveway. It took Emma a moment to realize who it was. She reached for Tiffany's arm, "What is he doing driving? He just got out of the hospital today!"

"It looks like someone is with him." Ryan had Pastor Cross with him. "He must be eager to get things settled." She looked Emma head on, "Be honest with him Sis. Lay it all out there on the table. Let him see your heart, Emma. He was your husband."

"You know, I never could call him my ex-husband."

"What does that tell you about your heart?"

"He is still a part of me."

The knock on the back door caused them to both look at that direction. "Go with that then Emma. Let God guide you. You will be alright."

There was another knock on the door as they embraced again.

"Thank you, Tiff. Love you."

Tiffany turned to the door and opened it up to her brother. She let out a little laugh at the dejected look he had on his face. "Hi there big brother. Good to see you again." He leaned down to hug her. She whispered in his ear, "Be patient and go slow."

"Got it little sister. Man it is good to hug you!" He squeezed her a little tighter, winced as they both forgot for a moment of his injury, and then let her go. She patted him on the back as she walked past him while he walked in the house to find Emma. He didn't have to look for long she was sitting on her lounge chair in the corner of the room. "Is it safe to come in?" She was looking out the window, wondering if it was alright to let him in, and not just into her house.

She heard his boots walk across the floor in her direction. If she was honest with herself, she would realize that she was afraid to look at him. She was afraid of the flood of emotion that would follow looking at the man that had held her heart since they were kids. She knew that he now stood next to her chair. She could feel his eyes on her, waiting, pleading for her to respond to him. Still looking out the window, she finally decided to say something. "Have a seat." She had not expected him to sit at her feet on the chair, but that is where he chose to sit.

"Honey, talk to me."

She whipped her head around, and stared him down. She took a deep breath to calm herself a bit and then let him have it.

"You are not to use any terms of endearment with me until we figure this out. I am not your 'Honey'! I am not anything to you right now besides the mother of your children. Is that clear?" She would not tell him that it felt good to hear him call her that again. To hear that word being directed at her from his lips was beautiful. She had to keep up the act until she had more answers. But she was finding it hard to keep up the act. He was sitting so close and was looking at her with all the love in the world in his eyes. She could see that he wanted her to love him and accept him again. She couldn't, not yet at least.

"Yes. No more pet names."

"Ryan. Tell me something, why?"

"I could give you a list of excuses, or I can give you honesty."

"Honesty is preferred."

"Okay, shame. I was ashamed."

"Of what?"

"My looks, my disabilities, the fact that I could no longer provide for you and the kids. I figured you could handle everything better without me mucking it all up with my injuries."

"You thought I could do it without you? Ryan, I was a mess. Do you know the hell you put me through?" Emma gave a cynical laugh, "No, of course you didn't know. You weren't here!" She yelled at him. She didn't stop there. "Ryan, you almost killed me! Stephen pulled away from everyone. Aaron was so confused he would stand by your side of the bed in the middle of the night and continue to ask where you were. I was so stressed; I couldn't feed our baby the way I was supposed to. Ann had to dress me and drag me from the house to feed me for a couple days after I got the divorce papers. Ryan! I was ready to die. You promised me forever, and you broke that promise."

There was silence. All they could hear was the hum of the fireplace. They stared at each other for what seemed like hours. The tension in the air was thick. Finally, Ryan broke the silence.

"Do you forgive me, Emma?"

She didn't know. She looked down at her hands. She couldn't look at him while she tried to figure it out. Her sister-in-law's words came back to her. *Be honest with him.* "I don't know Ryan. I want to. I also want to rewind the last eight years and keep you home from work. I want to go back and erase how harsh I was to you that day. But I can't, can I?"

"No you can't. We can't erase any of it. I wish I could go back too, but I can't. Now all we can do is move forward. So, how are we going to do that?"

"I don't know, but I do know, that I thank God this time wasn't as serious as last time you were in the hospital."

She watched Ryan get nervous now. He looked down at her feet. She could tell he wanted to say something, but she wasn't sure she wanted him to. The look of uneasiness in his eyes turned to a look that she only seen in their most private moments when they were married. It had been a long time since she had seen this look in his eyes, and she was not sure she was ready to see it again. She could feel it melt the wall that she had built around herself.

"Ryan, I want you to be honest, but the look you are giving me..."

He broke off her words by running his finger down the slope of the top of her foot. She could feel the air catch in her chest. He clearly remembered all the way he could get her to calm down and get out of her head. "Emma, the last three weeks, well four weeks now, have been amazing. I don't want our time together to end just because you know the truth." He looked up at her at that moment.

"Ryan, I don't think..."

"Emma, stop thinking for a second and listen to what I am saying. I want us to be a family again. I still love you. I never stopped. I tried, God knows I tried but I can't run from it anymore." His voice was so quiet that she had to lean toward him to hear him. "Emma, I want to see us fix this. I want to love you again. So I ask you, do you forgive me?"

She couldn't think. Her emotions confused her. She wanted to lean over and wrap her arms around him and shout yes from the tree tops but she wasn't a school girl anymore. She was an adult, a mother. She bowed her head and was looking at her hands again, but she could also feel him lightly stroking the tops of her feet. She sat there, enjoying the sensation of Ryan touching her again. Then the thought came to mind, *What God has brought together, let no man tear apart.* The peace that followed after that made her realize that she had her answer. It was a risk to let him back into her heart and she found that she was truly willing to let him in. She had just been so afraid to let him in that the real desire of her heart was being over shadowed.

No more fear. Only love and forgiveness.

With a deep breath, she leaned forward, and took his hand in hers. She looked up at him just in time to see the surprise in his eyes, and in the same hushed tone as he had been talking to her, said "Ryan, I can't think or talk when you do that." They smiled at each other in realization that he still had that effect on her.

"I am glad. I want this to go in my favor."

He said this with a slight chuckle.

Still smiling, she proceeded to try to put a sentence or two together. "Ryan, I do forgive you. I do still love you. Even when I was angry, I loved you."

An idea came to her mind. The thought made the butterflies in her stomach begin to dance, but she knew it was something she had to do.

She shifted her body closer to his. She got a kick out of his look of surprise, yet again. Clearly he figured I would stay seated in one spot. *Just you wait big guy, I am not done yet.* She then reached her hand up toward the right side of his face. He flinched a bit. She hesitated just a little bit but then the palm of her hand found his cheek. The weight of it was feather light. "Emma? What are you doing?"

Even though she was touching the side of his face that was scarred and rippled from the cuts and burns, it felt so good to touch him again.

"Ryan, it is okay. I just need to touch you. It has been eight long years. I am realizing how much I have missed this. I need to be reminded of what you feel like. And I need to learn the feel of you now."

He leaned his head into her hand ever so slightly. It was like a fresh rain, washing all the hurt and pain away. He then reached up and did the same and put his hand on her cheek, and she leaned into his hand as well. "God I hate that we aren't married, right now."

She gave him an understanding smile.

"I won't stay long. You have me feeling like a teenager again right now. In fact, the other night, watching the fierce 'warrior princess' come out in you again brought back a lot of memories. They haven't stopped since. So close and yet so far. That's where we are right now."

"I know but we have to be careful. It would be so easy."

At that moment, Ryan bent his head forward so that their foreheads touched. "Emma?"

"Yes."

"Can I kiss you?"

"I wish you would."

Consent given, he placed his other hand on the other side of her face, winced from the sharp pain in his side, looked her in the eyes, and leaned in. He touched his lips to hers with a feather light touch. She could hear both of them inhale and then they both held their breath. It didn't take long to remember how good it felt to kiss him. It had always been electric and nothing had changed. She wrapped her arms around his neck as he turned just enough so they could get a little closer. He then wrapped his arms around her and they held on to each other. That's when the light and easy kissing became deeper and more intense. Their breathing increased and the old warmth of his passionate kisses washed over them. It would be so easy to forget that they were not married. But before she could reluctantly pull away, he did the same. Their foreheads met again and he let out a rush of air.

"Oh sweetie, I guess I will have to leave sooner than planned. I am so glad we didn't forget how to do that." He placed his finger just under her chin and tilted her head up so she could look at him. "Now that I have you back in my life, I don't want to let you go. Knowing that this monster before you doesn't bother you, makes me hate wasting all those years. I should have trusted you and what we had. Please forgive me."

Emma could feel the pressure build behind her eyes until the dam broke and overflowed and ran down her cheeks. "Ryan, I told you, you are forgiven. Let's just move forward."

Ryan kissed her again, but broke the kiss almost as quick as he had started it. "Mmmm, yeah I can't keep doing that. Not until we decide on what to do next." That brought out a little giggle.

"Ryan, you promised me forever, I am going to hold you to it."

With a smile, he agreed. He kissed the tip of her nose and hesitantly walked to the door. "Is it safe for me to assume that we need to call Pastor Cross and go to the courthouse and file for that wonderful piece of paper in the next week?"

"Maybe." She gave him her cutest smile and a wink.

He rushed back to her and took her in his arms. He winced in pain, again. "How about we wait until I heal?" She nodded through her laughter. He began to kiss her all over her face. It made her laugh hysterically with joy.

"Baby I love you!!!!" he whispered as his lips hovered over hers.

"I am never letting you go again" she replied.

Epilogue

The kids had their dad and she had her husband back. He had come to the house first thing in the morning for breakfast, helped get the kids off to school, and was there at the end of the day and stayed until bedtime. Sarah refused to leave his side. Aaron was saying "dad" every time he talked to Ryan. Stephen would sit as close to Ryan as possible when they watched TV on the couch. Emma had a hard time getting any alone time with him.

Emma and Ryan married during the following Christmas Eve service at their church. Pastor Cross had insisted they go through marriage counseling again because there was so much that they had to confront before they should marry again. They didn't want to go into their marriage again with so much hurt and pain hanging over them.

The boys stood with Ryan and Sarah stood with Emma. It was a beautiful candlelight service that night and it was one no one would ever forget.

Today was the ten-year anniversary of the accident that rocked their worlds and changed everything for Emma and Ryan and eighteen months since Ryan came back into their lives. As Emma stood at the sink doing dishes, she rubbed the small of her back to work out the kink. Just two more months and a new addition would be joining their family. She was glad they had decided to keep her house and sell his place. They were going to need the room.

While she was rubbing her low back, she felt a big, strong hand touch the spot she was trying to ease and Ryan took over massaging her back. "Mmmm. That feels like heaven. You can stop that next year."

"How about in just a couple of months."

"Sounds good to me."

"Penny for your thoughts."

"Thinking about what today is. Thanking God for bringing it all back together."

"I am glad we followed His crumb trail."

"I am too. Of course, He made it pretty easy for the kids and I to come back to town. All doors but this one here were slammed shut."

"I am blessed to have you back in my life, Emma. I kick myself for being such a fool."

Emma turned around to face him, took both of his wrists and wrapped his arms around her so they could stand as close as her round belly would allow. She then placed her hand on both sides of his face, stroking his scarred side with her thumb.

"Don't ever, ever beat yourself up over that again. We are together, we are married again, the kids are happy, and..." she took one of his hands and placed it on her belly, "we are increasing our family. What more could we ask for? I am just happy to have you with me again."

"You're right, God has truly blessed us. He never let us forget each other and He kept guiding us back to this place. I am so glad to have you and the kids back in my life. I am a blessed man."

He bent over to kiss her softly. At that moment, the kids walked into the kitchen. Emma and Ryan were not aware of having an audience until they heard the harmonizing sound of "EEEWWW!"

Ryan pulled back with a chuckle, but did not let Emma out of his embrace. While they lovingly looked into each other's eyes, Aaron took that moment to say, "Aren't you two a little old for that?"

Ryan wiggled his eye brows up and down as he looked at Emma with a devilish grin and replied, "Nothing wrong with a little kitchen fire, right dear?" Emma and Ryan broke out into laughter and kissed each other as another round of "Eeeewwww's" rose up to the ceiling.

God had brought back together what man had tried to pull apart and they were blessed for following His lead.

What God Brings Together

Melissa resides in a small mid-Michigan farm community with her husband and three children, all of whom they home school. Besides writing, she enjoys reading, taking photos, and motorcycle rides with her husband. Her hope is that each story touches your heart, gives you hope, or just gives you a moment away from the chaos of life.

<u>Books by Melissa Wardwell</u>
(and more to come)

Promises from Above Series
What God Brings Together – December 2014
Dance and Be Glad – June 2016
I Know the Plans – Coming Soon
Redeemed by Grace – Coming Soon

Brides of Promise Novella Series
A Christmas Wedding – November 2015

Finding Hope in Savannah – September 2015

<u>Where to Find Melissa Wardwell</u>
www.melissawardwell.com
www.facebook.com/mwardwell99
www.twitter.com/mwardwell99
melissawardwell_author – on Instagram
www.pinterest.com/MWardwell99/

What God Brings Together

Made in the USA
Middletown, DE
16 July 2016